SYDNEY SCOTT

EVERNIGHT PUBLISHING ®

www.evernightpublishing.com

Copyright© 2024

Sydney Scott

ISBN: 978-0-3695-1065-5

Cover Artist: Jay Aheer

Editor: Lisa Petrocelli

SYDNEY SCOTT

DEDICATION

For my amazing siblings. Thank you for your love, your laughter, and your support.

SYDNEY SCOTT

WITH THIS WISH

Starlight Lake, 1

Sydney Scott

Copyright © 2024

Then

Chapter One
Maya

The sound of metal cutting wood greets me as I walk toward the converted storage shed, the smell of sawdust hitting my nose and the noise growing steadily louder with each step I take that brings me closer to my brother's workspace. When I finally make it to the open side door, I peek my head around the corner as inconspicuously as possible as to not spook my brother while he works with his power tools. Carter has his large, noise-canceling headphones on to block the buzzing sounds that echo around the small space, but even with that one sense blocked he is still very aware of his surroundings. I know that if he catches even a glimpse of me out of the corner of his eye, he's going to jump right out of his skin and possibly cause a small accident, or worse, a not-so-small one. Carter is easily startled to an almost comical extent. It probably has to do with all the thriller and mystery novels he reads, something he should probably change since there's no way he'll give up his profession as a woodworker anytime soon.

Woodworking was a trade Carter learned from our father, Stellan Johansen. The Norwegian Viking of a man had tried teaching me as well, and while I can still probably put together a pretty decent cutting board or footstool, I haven't ever been nearly as talented or as interested in the trade as Carter always was. Instead, I chose to focus mainly on the acquisition side of the business. Hodgepodge, the aptly named space where we sell a varied collection of goods and furnishings, has been around for decades. Years ago, our maternal grandfather started the business, bringing together items from local artisans, craftsman, and vendors to sell in one place to the people of Starlight Lake, Colorado, as well as members of other surrounding mountain communities and tourists of the area. Our mom, Olive, worked at the shop from the time she was a teenager, manning the cash register and interacting with the customers. At the age of twenty-two, she met our dad when he traveled to the store to sell his hand-carved chairs, stools, and benches. According to both our parents, it was love at first sight, and after a whirlwind romance, they married and had Carter less than a year later.

Ours were the greatest parents any two kids could ask for. They were endlessly supportive of my and Carter's endeavors, even when I decided to pursue a major in Art History my freshman year of college in Boulder. Sadly, that degree is incomplete, the space on the wall in the office for my diploma as empty as my desire to finish my studies. My senior year at Boulder University didn't quite go as planned, with Mom and Dad getting killed in a fatal car accident derailing everything. It was late fall, and I only had a couple of weeks of classes left before I would head home for winter break when I got the call from Carter that would forever alter the course of my life. *Our* lives. That call is seared into my memory. As much as I try to forget the sound of my brother's broken voice as he said the words I can never forget, it's the same sound I felt in my heart the minute his words registered. I don't think I'll ever be able to erase that call from my mind. Time continues to pass, but the memory remains.

"Maya, it's Mom and Dad." The echo of Carter's voice comes flying back from the past and I rub at the pain in my chest at the thought of that night. Who would have thought I would go from sitting in my dorm room, hanging out with my roommate, to packing my bags and moving home for good? I had to do it. Carter and I were all the other had left, and truthfully, after your parents die, finishing college just doesn't seem that important anymore. As if that hadn't been enough change for one lifetime, about three weeks after our parents' car was run off the icy mountain road by a drunk driver, Carter and I got more bad news. Our parents had taken out a second mortgage on their house to cover recent renovations to the store, leaving Carter and I with the choice of either trying to take over the monthly payments ourselves, or selling our childhood home. I remember Carter and I looking at each other dumbfounded when our parents' lawyer, Mr. Barnaby, delivered the news.

"What does this mean for us?" Carter had asked incredulously. "I thought Dad paid off the house a long time ago?"

The lawyer shook his head sadly. "It was still a

few years from being paid off, and your father took out a second mortgage a few months back," he informed us.

"Why?" I asked. "Why would Dad do that?" Their dad would never have risked their childhood home for a new paint job.

Barnaby simply shrugged. "It seems there were some repairs needed after termites were discovered a year or so ago. I'm guessing your father figured he would do a total refresh on the business while he was at it, but that's only a guess. We can't really know his motivations."

Right, because he was gone now. My head turned to my brother, and I gawked at him, still in shock. "Did you know about any of this?"

My brother's red-rimmed eyes met mine. "I knew about the termite damage and needing to fix it, but I had no idea about any of the money stuff." He sniffled and wiped at his wet eyes with the sleeve of his flannel. "I've just been working on building things, Mai. I didn't know anything about the house."

"I can't believe they didn't say anything." How could neither of us have known about this?

He shook his head. "You were at school, I live above the store. They didn't really have a reason to tell us anything about the house," he said quietly.

I turned back to Barnaby. "What are our options?" I had asked, panicked at the thought of losing the house Carter and I grew up in. We created so many happy memories there and I couldn't imagine losing the space that held them.

The lawyer gathered up his papers and tapped them on the kitchen table where we held the meeting. "Well, you can take over the payments yourself..." he had started, but when he saw the look of despair on our faces, he cut himself off with a sigh. "Then you'll have to sell it to pay back the bank. If you're lucky, there might be enough left over to do something nice for yourselves."

"Like what?" I asked with a snort. "We can't buy new parents." I winced at my snarky tone and looked up at the man apologetically. "Sorry."

"No, I'm sorry. I wish you both the best," he told us. He shoved the papers in his briefcase and turned to leave, barely noticing that he just ruined our world for a second time in a month.

A splintering sound rockets me from the difficulties of the past and back to the present. I shake my head to clear away the unpleasant memories and walk toward my brother, watching as he curses under his breath before tossing the split wood into his scrap pile. Now that he's at a break in his work, I can do what I came here to do. My fingers reach up and tap lightly on Carter's shoulder, trying to touch as little of his sweat-soaked t-shirt as possible.

My brother reaches up and pulls his headphones off from the top of his damp hair. "What's up, Mai?" he asks, using the nickname he's had for me since the day I was born. Even though we're both in our twenties, Carter still calls me Mai in just about every situation. Whenever he uses my full name, though, I know something is wrong.

"Not much," I say, passing over the cool bottle of water I snagged from the office mini-fridge. My fingers tap against the side of my wool leggings as I muster up the courage to ask him my question. "So, what are you working on?" That's not the question I want to ask, but it's a whole lot easier than the other one.

Carter wipes some sweat from his brow. Despite it being November and the temperature in the mid-forties, the garage is warm and Carter seems to have been at it since early this morning. He was always a hard worker, but since our parents passed, he's been more singularly focused on his projects. "Well, I *was* attempting to curve the wood for the back of a rocking chair, but the damn thing split on me," he grumbles. He pulls off his work gloves and runs his hand through his hair, the brown darker than normal due to how damp it is. "I just can't seem to do anything right today."

Carter's inability to focus isn't surprising seeing as how tomorrow is the second anniversary of our parents' passing. Last year, Carter had spent the anniversary camping out near the lake in quiet retrospection while I spent it with our Aunt Sue, distracting ourselves from our grief by reminiscing about the good times we had with them before they left us. Sue isn't our aunt by blood, but she was Mom's best friend since they were little and has always been a part of our lives in some small way. She lives in Los Angeles now, working as a successful salesperson. Sue is always busy, but she makes time for us, coming back to visit a couple of times a year. It's not the same as having Mom here, but it helps.

The toe of my boot scuffs at the concrete floor as I gaze around the workshop. It would be easy to make more small talk to avoid the inevitable, but I've put it off long enough. "Hey, Car?" When my brother's moss-green eyes meet mine, I can see just how tired they are. We both have a hard time sleeping this time of year. I had hoped things would get better for the two of us with time, but it seems that two years hasn't been enough. "Will you come to the holiday lighting with me tonight?"

The Starlight Lake holiday lighting ceremony is something we always used to do as a family. Each year in early November, the citizens of Starlight Lake gather in the town square to countdown the moments before the mayor flips a switch that turns on thousands of white twinkle lights strung up in trees and on buildings throughout the downtown area. The lights themselves are beautiful, but it's the spectacle and the comradery of gathering with hundreds of other people that my family and I enjoyed most. We attended every year. Once the shop was closed, our parents would take us to dinner at the local café and then we'd walk toward the town square, stopping at the large fountain to toss in a penny and make a wish for the upcoming year. After that, we would grab a hot chocolate from the coffee cart and wait with the rest of the townspeople for the lights to come on, listening to local bands play holiday music as people danced and sang along. Those nights were magical, and while it was too painful to attend last year, I'm ready to go and be a part of things again. We've been putting our lives on hold long enough.

"Come on, Carter," I beg my brother, but by the fixed stare on his face, I can tell my plea is falling on deaf ears. "Please?"

He's already shaking his head and turning his attention back to his project. "Sorry, Mai. I'm really behind on a few things and then I'm going camping later." He grips the edge of the table tightly, his posture stiff for a moment before he looks over his shoulder at me. "I'm just not ready yet," he breathes out, his expression pained.

In two quick steps, I'm at my brother's side, wrapping my arms around him to give him comfort and let him know that even though I would love to have him with me, I understand better than anyone just how much pain he's dealing with. We all grieve differently, and I won't rush him no matter how much his being there would mean to me. Carter takes a deep breath and pats my back. "Maybe next year," he tells me, but I won't hold him to it. The memories tied to the lighting festival are special. I don't want to risk tainting them.

"That would be nice," I tell him, giving him one more squeeze before releasing him to go open the shop. I make my way to the door, but pause to give Carter one last smile. "How about you join me for lunch later? We can eat at the counter while people shop."

Carter smiles sadly at me and nods. "That sounds nice."

"Great. Egg salad sandwiches are on me," I tell him. I enjoy the sound of his light laughter as I make my way out of the shed and cross the small expanse into the back door of Hodgepodge. The new look of the store is an ever-present reminder of why I now live in the space above the shop with Carter, but I have to admit the renovations my parents were willing to sacrifice our house for at least turned out nicely. Where there were once stark-white walls, cement flooring, and simple display cases, customers are now greeted with dark-gray walls, built-in shelving, birchwood floors that shine in the light pouring through the large front window, and new displays in a variety of shapes and materials. We not only display items from local artisans, but we take old items and make them new again. I wish someone could make me new again and give me that sense of belonging and family I've longed for the last two years. A small smile pulls across my face as I flip the sign on the front door to show that we're now open. I think I just found my fountain wish for this year's ceremony, and if my parents are watching over me like I think they are, it just might have a chance of coming true.

Chapter Two
Jake

The sun is shining, the air is crisp and clean, and large swaths of evergreen trees greet me as I wind my way through the Rocky Mountains back to Denver. It's a perfect fall day, but I couldn't be more miserable if I tried. Well, that last part may be an exaggeration, but I'm in a bit of a mood today. I'm not always so grouchy, but transitions are hard for me, even when it's in order to fulfill the life plan I mapped out for myself a decade ago.

While it was one hundred percent my choice to leave my job in Seattle to work for my dad in Denver, I can't help but feel a little irritated at the disruption in my routine. My life in Seattle was decent, and I liked working at Seattle Sustainable Solutions. After graduating with my MBA from Washington State, I was immediately hired and started as a low-level marketing consultant for the company, and after three years, I was really starting to make a name for myself. Even though my job didn't leave me a lot of time to socialize, I made sure to attend happy hours with my colleagues and joined a few pickup soccer games to stave off any loneliness I felt due to a lack of dating prospects. Dating apps have never really been my thing. No one would ever call me a romantic, but I have always thought I would meet someone randomly and we would just click. Perhaps that's just wishful thinking, or maybe I'm not being realistic about how things work nowadays.

"Jake is a man with a plan." That's what my friends in high school and college would say to me. And it was true. My whole life has been planned out, first by my parents, and then by me. Alexander and Shelly Mackenzie have always been big on routine, and that

extended to how they raised their son. From the moment I was born, I had a routine for everything. There was my feeding schedule, my nap schedule, my bedtime routine. Every moment of my young life ran according to plan. As I aged, the routines changed slightly, but they were still always there. School, soccer, clarinet lessons, homework, and meals all happened at a specific time and in a specific order. That lifestyle continued as I went off to college. I kept a strict schedule of classes and work, making sure to balance it out by socializing with classmates and dating. The girls that managed to hang on for more than a few weeks eventually grew tired of my inflexibility and routine, and I happily said goodbye, wanting to find someone who clicked with me exactly as I was. Admittedly, I was a lot more rigid my first two years than I was after that and in graduate school, but by then I was too busy to care much about dating. A life that predictable may drive some people crazy, but I thrived off the knowledge that certain things would happen at certain times and every move I made was part of a greater plan. It took choice out of the equation, but that never bothered me.

Even now, as I continue the long drive from my old apartment in Seattle to my new one in Denver, I can't help but feel like the choice I've made to follow my life's plan is the right one. My senior year of high school, I came up with the blueprint for the rest of my life. The plan was to graduate high school, do my undergrad and graduate studies at Washington State, then work at a smaller firm until my dad opened a position for me at his company in Colorado. Mile High Consulting is extremely successful and much sought after by large companies when it comes to business marketing, finance, technology, security, you name it. My dad started the company with his friend, Anton Kochev, and the two grew it from a start-up to a multimillion-dollar enterprise in just twenty-five years. While I have no doubt I can work well there, I'm more interested in helping small businesses like I had in Washington. I can't just turn around and go back there, though. After giving my notice, they hired someone right away, even asking me to train the guy. The lease on my apartment was broken too, so I wouldn't even have a place to live immediately. Besides, staying there long-term was never part of the plan, and that is something I have always been committed to. With a curt nod to myself as a reminder that the plan is what matters, I drive on toward my destiny.

The sound of a call coming through the Bluetooth speaker draws my attention to the screen on the dash, and I smile at the name flashing at me. "Billie," I exclaim to my friend of over twenty years. "Calling to welcome me home?"

Biliyana Kochev is the daughter of my father's business partner and my best friend in the world. The two of us were practically raised as brother and sister, though where I was raised on the strictest of schedules, Billie was what is commonly referred to as a "free-range kid." Where she went and when didn't really concern her parents as long as she was safe and not getting in too much trouble, which almost always was the case except for a few times in high school when she discovered her rebellious side. Covering the boy's locker room in toilet paper our junior year and sneaking a flask filled with vodka into prom among her more notable crimes, though there were others. While I was busy keeping my head down and making plans, Billie was pushing boundaries and ruling over the school with her mix of wild ideas and genuine friendliness toward everyone. Most people still see her as a bit of a "party girl," but she's not that. She never has been really, but people don't always look very closely.

The sound of a soft snort coming through the speaker brings me back to my friend. "Please. I've had much better things to do than sit around waiting for you to show your ugly mug," she tells me, her voice teasing.

I chuckle at the harmless insult. "Come on. You know you missed me," I say, making another turn through the mountain passage. I know for a fact that my friend will be happy to see me. We talked all the time when I lived in Seattle, but her calls have gotten more frequent the closer we've come to my return date. "Who else keeps you in check like I do?"

"No one. That's what makes you're coming back such a bummer," she says, but I can hear the smile in her voice. "Since you bring it up, does that mean you plan on coming with me to keep me out of trouble? It's been a while since we went clubbing. I'm not sure you can handle it."

"I would dispute that, but there is no doubt in my mind that if we did go out, you would run circles around me." While Billie lives to go out and have a good time, I've always been more of a homebody. Being around that many people at once makes me a little anxious and trying to get to know someone one-on-one with an incessant bass line pounding through your ears isn't exactly easy either.

"That I would," she says proudly. I hear chewing on the other end of the phone and my stomach growls in reply. Breakfast was a long time ago and I haven't eaten since then. It's coming up on two o'clock and there's no way I will make it to dinner without grabbing something. My eyes flick to a sign on the side of the road for a town and I decide a little rest stop wouldn't put me too far behind schedule. "I called to ask if I could take you out for a belated birthday celebration. I know I called last week, but now that you're back we can go somewhere fun."

"I don't know, Billie," I tell her hesitantly. "I kind of want to just focus on getting settled in." As hard as it is to transition to a new stage in life, it's got to be done and the sooner I get started the better.

"Please," she whines, and I can picture the pouty face she busts out whenever she wants to get her way. "We can totally do something your speed. I hear the senior living community down the street has the best boiled potatoes in the city. I'll even throw in a bag of ribbon candy as extra incentive."

"Very nice," I say dryly. Billie loves to poke fun at me, but I know she likes things more low-key most of the time too. It seems she's just determined to play the role she created for herself when we were younger and pretend she's all about partying. "We can definitely do dinner tomorrow, but right now I'm thinking about lunch. I'm going to grab some food before I head back on the road."

"Fine, go feed your face," she says with a chuckle. "Call me tomorrow and I can help you get settled in your apartment before we go out to dinner."

"By help me get settled, you really mean go through my clothes and make fun of my wardrobe, don't you?" Billie loves to give me shit at every opportunity, especially when it comes to how I dress. I don't see anything wrong with my jeans and sweatshirts, but apparently they're not up to snuff.

"One hundred percent," she sings to me. "See you soon, Jake."

"Bye, Billie." I end the call and shake my head at my friend. Billie is someone I will love until the day I die, but sometimes her jokes hit a sore spot that I wish she would just leave alone. So what if I wear the same thing all the time? It's not a big deal, though now that I'm at a more prestigious firm, I'm going to have to step up my fashion game. No doubt Billie will volunteer to help me with that. The thought of having to go shopping at all makes me groan, but luckily I'm saved from having to think about it any longer when I see my turnoff.

Flicking on my turn signal, I exit the Interstate and make my way toward the small town of Starlight Lake. The name of the town sounds like a place from a children's bedtime story, and I half expect to run into fairies and ogres as I drive into town. "Oh, wow," the sentiment escapes my mouth without permission as I take in the sight before me. Nestled in a small green valley is Starlight Lake. The tree-covered mountains make a beautiful backdrop and are reflected in what looks to be a crystal-clear lake at the base. As I get closer, red brick buildings line the street that cuts through the center of town, and I turn my head slightly to check out the people walking along, shopping, or out sweeping in front of their businesses. It looks idyllic, and while I'm not a big believer in magic, if it did exist, it would probably be in a place like this.

After soaking in as much of the town as I can from the car, I pull into a parking space in front of an eatery called Fran's Place, at least I'm assuming it's an eatery based off the sandwich board advertising specials on the sidewalk out front. With one last look around, I hop out of my SUV and head into the café. The walls are pink and white with matching booths lining them and a long, black counter running in front of an open window into the kitchen. Black-and-white photographs are scattered over the walls depicting a time long since passed but one that is clearly held in esteem by the owners. A place like this could easily look dated or kitsch, but instead it evokes a sense of nostalgia. For what, I'm not sure, but even though I probably won't like much on the menu, I find myself drawn further into the space, finally taking an open seat at the counter.

A woman breezes by, dropping off a glass of water and a menu, acknowledging me with a simple, "Be right with you," before she's off to the other end of the café.

"Thanks," I mumble, far too late for her to hear me. Opening the menu, I scan the list of items in search of anything that will fit my eating plan. Food isn't something I necessarily restrict, but I like to exercise and eat to fuel my body, only occasionally veering off my meal plan. I also don't have a lot of time or the inclination to cook, so I rely on meal prep services. I ask for lean, nutritionally dense breakfasts, lunches, and dinners. Nothing on this menu seems to fit that description, but to quell the intense growling in my stomach, I can make due. The smell of crisp potatoes and salt hits my noise and my eyes wander over to the plate of the person next to me. My mouth immediately starts watering at the sight of the man's French fries and my stomach protests even louder than before. Sadly, as much as I'd like to partake in some fried food, I don't want to deal with any negative side effects when I get back on the road.

"All right, hon. What'll it be?" I look up, seeing that my waitress is back, pen in hand ready to jot my order down on her pad.

With one final glance at the menu, I pick the item that's most like what I normally eat. "I'll have the grilled chicken salad with a vinaigrette on the side, please."

Her pen scribbles quickly, and she peers at me momentarily. "Anything to drink?"

My eyes flick to the water glass to make sure it looks potable before I commit to anything, but it's as crystal clear as the lake outside. "I'm good with water, thanks."

"Great," she says, ripping off the slip of paper and spinning around to slide it across the barrier between the dining area and kitchen. "That'll be right up."

Ten minutes later, I'm poking my fork around the dish in front of me. When I looked over the menu, I kind of knew what I was getting into food wise, but apparently I wasn't quite as prepared as I thought I was. The grilled chicken salad seemed like the least innocuous item on the menu and I figured, hey, you can't mess up a salad, but the contents of the bowl that's currently staring me in the face is not what I'm used to. "Excuse me," I say, flagging down my waitress. "Could you tell me why there's cheese in my salad?"

The older woman with her faded black hair tied into a bun gives me a questioning look. "Because it comes with cheese," she says before turning to help another customer, but I call out before she can get too far.

"But I ordered the grilled chicken salad," I say, as if that should explain why I am having an internal crisis at the appearance of yellow strings of dairy sprinkled atop iceberg lettuce. I give another cursory poke with my fork and frown at it. I've had cheese in salad before, like feta or blue cheese, but never this. "Is this cheddar?"

The woman, who is clearly over my pickiness, drops the coffeepot she was wielding on the warmer behind her and reaches over to pat my hand. I look into her warm brown eyes and am shocked to not see annoyance, but patience and understanding in her expression instead. "It is cheddar, and it comes in every salad. If you're lactose intolerant or truly prefer to not have it in there, I can bring you another, but I assure you that if you try it, you'll like it," she promises. Her smile is pleasant, and I decide to not make too big of a fuss.

With a shrug of my shoulder, I grab the side of vinaigrette I requested and give her a smile. "Why not? I can take a walk on the wild side," I tell her. Before I can pour it over my salad, she stops me with a hand on my forearm and a slow shake of her head.

"Oh, honey. If cheese on salad is the wild side, you need to do a whole lot more living," she tells me with a sad smile before reaching the counter behind her and grabbing another bottle. She plops it in front of me and I see that it's ranch dressing, something I'm not sure I've ever tried in my entire life. "Use this instead. It'll really blow your mind." With a wink, she grabs her coffeepot and heads over to refill mugs for some of the other patrons.

I eye the bottle skeptically, but decide that in the spirit of trying new things, I'll go for it. With a small smile at myself for stretching my comfort zone, I take the bottle and drizzle the creamy white liquid on my salad. Grabbing my fork, I take a little of everything into my mouth and groan as the spicy dressing and creaminess of the cheese hit my tongue. The chicken tastes perfectly grilled too, but it takes a back seat to the other more robust flavors hitting me as I chew. This foray into the wider culinary universe is proving to not be all bad, and I continue to eat my salad, making a mental note to add ranch dressing to my grocery list.

My server reappears and gives me a once-over, a slow grin playing at the corners of her mouth. "How's the wild side treating you, hon?" she asks, handing me a napkin and gesturing to my chin.

I accept the cloth and wipe a glob of dressing from my face, nodding in thanks. "It's not as scary as I thought it would be," I admit with a smile. My eyes once again flick over to the fries on the plate near to me. They look good, and clearly this place has quality stuff since my salad is turning out better than I thought. I decide to throw my usual self-imposed dietary requirements out the window and just go after what I want. "Could I get an order of fries, please?"

The woman, who if my peek at her name tag is any indication, is the titular Fran who owns the cafe, smiles knowingly before reaching behind her to grab a small plate of golden sticks that look fresh from the fryer. "I had a feeling you might be wanting some of these," she says, her eyes crinkling in the corners.

Blinking at her in disbelief, I huff a breath. "Are you a mind reader or something?" I ask, pulling the plate toward me and grabbing the ketchup bottle on the counter.

Her expression turns wistful. "Some people like to think so," she says, giving me a small wink. "They go on and on about how this town is magic and that I must have gotten my powers of clairvoyance from drinking lake water or something." She sighs and her head shakes to clear away the memory. "In reality, I'm just good at reading people, and I could tell it had been a while since you gave yourself permission to go after what you really wanted."

I lean back in the vinyl stool, oddly unsettled by her astute assessment of me. "What gave you that impression?"

Fran's shoulder shrugs nonchalantly and her easy smile returns. "Not sure really. Maybe it's all tourists who come through here, but there just seems to be something a little more buckled up about people from the city. It's like you all are so busy making plans for your lives that you don't take the time to live it."

"Wow," I tell her, scratching my head. My finger snags on a rogue curl and I make a mental note to get my hair trimmed before I start at the office on Monday. "You really are good at reading people."

"Maybe," she says, her voice slow as molasses as she leans an elbow on the counter between us. "Or maybe I just think that a life that's all hustle and bustle with no breaks for the little things, isn't much of a life. Time is too fleeting to not spend it doing things that make us happy. Things like skipping stones in the lake, or gazing up at the stars on a clear night, or..." She points at the salad I have almost entirely eaten and smiles. "Or eating salad with cheese and ranch."

My exhale is slow as I think about everything she just said. "While there is definitely not much cause to stargaze in the city, I don't know that it's all that different from here." I was happy in Seattle, and enjoyed growing up in Denver. Didn't I? As my mind sifts through memories of the past, the answer to that question becomes less and less certain. I thought I was happy, but the more I sit here and stare at my plate I fries, I wonder if maybe I've simply been going through the motions, following the plan for my life instead of living it.

"Maybe not, but I can still tell when someone needs to let loose a little, and you, Mister No Cheese on Salad, need to let loose," she says. "I don't know how long you're in town, but you should take in the sights, hit some of the stores. You never know. You might just end up enjoying yourself a little." With a polite nod, she pulls back to her full height before turning on her heel and walking down the counter to start chatting up another patron.

After polishing off my salad, every fry on my plate, and paying my bill, I decide to head into town and get a look at the other local businesses. Maybe it will be a colossal waste of time, but maybe Fran was right and I'll end up enjoying myself a little. The cool air hits my face as I exit the café and I glance around, taking a deep breath and enjoying the invigorating feel of the fresh mountain air as it fills my lungs. Looking around for my next destination, I spot a turquoise awning with the word "Hodgepodge" written in white letters staring at me from across the street. My body feels oddly drawn to the small shop. Hodgepodge could literally mean anything, but I feel compelled to go there. It seems like as good a place as any to start my little adventure, so I head over, hoping to enjoy myself for little while before my plans start calling again.

Chapter Three
Maya

Lunch with Carter went better than expected. After our conversation in the workshop earlier, I fully expected the meal we shared behind the counter, as tourists wandered in and out of the shop, to be nothing but awkward, stilted conversation, but it was surprisingly good. My brother apologized for not going to the lighting festival with me, and after telling him no apology was necessary, we spoke a little about our plans for the evening and following day. Carter, of course, plans to pack a bag and camp out near the lake, no doubt staring up at the stars and talking to our dad like I know he does when he thinks no one is watching. They were close, bonded by a love of the same craft and an inexplicable love of brunost, a Norwegian cheese byproduct they would put on waffles. The two of them tried to convince me it tasted like caramel, and while it's not horrible, it doesn't compare to the real thing. My mom didn't like it either, so the two of us stuck to the more traditional waffle topping of maple syrup. She and I had a similar closeness that Carter and my dad seemed to have, but instead of bonding over woodworking and foreign food, we would go looking for artisans to feature in the store and she would tell me all about how the town was filled with magic.

My mother was a fanciful person. She believed in the inherent good in others and that magic existed in ways that most people didn't realize. Her superstitions were few, but she always believed that putting good out into the world came back to you, and that making a wish in the fountain at the town square would ensure it would come true. The first one always sounded nice, and I try to put good out into the world by being a polite, thoughtful, mostly positive person. I have been slacking on that front the last two years, losing myself in my grief a little too much to care about anything other than getting through the day, but I want to do better, even with things like my mom's idea of wishing in the fountain. Needing a little more magic in my life, I'm willing to try and believe it now. When I was younger, the whole thing was a little harder to swallow.

"I don't think that's true, Mommy," I had said to her when I was seven. "The fountain is broken. I wished for a pony and I didn't get one."

My mom just smiled and gave me a knowing look. "Didn't you, though?" she asked as we bundled together waiting for the holiday lights that year. "We went down to the Miller's Farm and you got to ride that small horse."

"But I didn't get to keep it," I argued, sniffling in the cold.

My mom rubbed her gloved hand up and down my back to reassure me. "The wish doesn't always come when or how you think it will, but it always comes," she told me.

From then I tried to keep track of my wishes and whether they came true in any form, but usually by the time January rolled around, I had forgotten all about the wish I made in November. As I grew up, I started just wishing to be happy, figuring that no matter how that wish came true, the result would be good. And I was happy ... for a while. When my parents died, I stopped wishing altogether. Attending the lighting festival was too painful, and it's difficult to believe in magic when the two people who loved you unconditionally are gone.

Our Aunt Sue called earlier today to check in since she won't be able to make it to town this year, and I consider her family, but she has her own life to worry about. She cares, I know she does, but it's not the same as having Mom and Dad here. My brother cares too, but he's going through the same trauma I am, and as close as we are, we're also different people. Where Carter needs more time, I'm ready to move on. Too much time was spent disappearing into myself, and I want to get back to who I used to be. That doesn't mean forgetting my parents, but instead I can honor them by living my life to the fullest.

The first part of doing that involves attending the lighting festival. This year, it will be a little different, not only because my parents aren't there, but because I contacted the local chapter of Mothers Against Drunk Driving and floated the idea of providing hot chocolate, apple cider, and cookies to people who come to the holiday lighting festival. The accident that killed my parents was caused by a drink driver, a man who had started drinking at the festival and kept the party going all the way through the next morning when he swerved into oncoming traffic, causing my parents to veer off the road and into a tree. The fact that my parents died on impact brings little solace. Even knowing that the man who drove under the influence was held responsible only brings the comfort of knowing he won't make the same mistake again. To prevent anyone else from having to lose a loved one, I thought that providing free drinks at the festival and having it sponsored by MADD could go a long way to helping me feel better, and I'm excited to volunteer tonight. When I'm done, I can watch the lights come on, enjoy the sights and people, and maybe I'll make that wish I thought of earlier. It's time to start living, and it might be time to start believing in magic again.

My eyes wander over to the clock on the screen of

the point-of-sale system and I see that I only have about two hours until closing. After that, it will be a quick wardrobe change and I'll be off to the festival. The customers have dwindled the later it gets, most people headed out to get ready for the lighting ceremony. With nothing to occupy my mind, I think about what my evening will be like, and the nerves settle in. My fingers fidget with the basket of woven bracelets on the counter as I try to calm the rattling feeling in my body, a combination of excitement and anxiety thrumming through me as I wait to attend the festival solo for the first time ever. My eyes blink away the moisture that threatens to fall at the thought of my parents not being there, and I touch the charm that rests on the chain around my neck to help center me. It's a silver valknut, or three interlocked triangles that represent family, and was something my father always wore around his neck up until the day he died. My finger traces the lines of the charm, letting the cool metal ground me as I take a few deep breaths. Just because they won't be there, doesn't mean they won't *be* there, I remind myself. No matter where I go, I carry them with me, and it's that thought I need to hold onto and find comfort in tonight.

Now that I'm feeling a little better, I start to tidy up behind the counter in anticipation of closing soon. Suddenly the bell above the shop door rings, drawing my attention to the front of the store. Putting on my best customer service smile, I look up to greet the customer, only for the words to get caught in my throat. The man stepping inside has to be the most handsome man I have ever laid eyes on. He's easily more than half a foot taller than my five foot six inches, and he has the most gorgeous auburn curls that fall to the nape of his neck. With a strong hand, he sweeps his hair back out of his face and I'm staring at chiseled features and a cleft chin resting in a strong jaw. He meanders around the store, picking up items here and there, inspecting them for a moment before placing them back gently. His obvious respect for the items is a nice change. Some people come in here like a bull in a china shop, but not this guy.

There is something vaguely familiar about him, but I can't place it. It's like I know him, or maybe I've just seen him somewhere before. Either way, he has this air about him that has me studying his movements, weirdly cataloging every detail. He glances around the shop for a moment, and when his gaze finally meets mine, I see a set of blue eyes a few shades darker than my own. Emotions I haven't felt in a long time clog my throat, so I swallow thickly, trying to find my voice.

"W-welcome to Hodgepodge," I say dumbly.

Usually I have a lot more pep in my greetings, but I'm still a little awestruck. Instant attraction to a man isn't something that normally happens to me, but there is something about this guy that's different, and it's not just his looks. When I look at him, I see a sense of stability, of safety, of permanence—all the things I've been missing the last two years. The stranger not only ticks all my boxes physically, but he seems to carry himself in a way that calls to me on some deeper level. My body feels grounded while my soul feels like it's about to take flight. If it weren't for the counter separating us, I can't be sure I wouldn't walk up and make a fool of myself by wrapping my arms around his neck and trying to kiss him.

The man's brow raises at my words and he smiles, his rosy lips pulling up at the corners. "Thank you," he says, wandering closer. I give him a once-over as he walks, taking note of the Washington State hoodie and formfitting jeans that hug his obviously athletic frame. The outfit is finished off with a pair of broken-in hiking boots, giving me a hint of at least one hobby. So, he's casual and outdoorsy, just my type. His head cocks to the side as his gaze narrows, his eyes filled with curiosity and mirth. "Do … do I know you?" he asks. A sigh of relief rushes from my lungs at knowing that I'm not going crazy because whatever I'm feeling, he seems to be feeling it too. "Never mind," he says quietly, dipping his head for a moment. "I think I would remember someone like you." My brows raise and my smile widens, but he keeps talking, probably trying to avoid any awkwardness. "What type of shop is this exactly?" His head spins around the store once again before he looks back at me.

Needing to get closer to this strangely familiar man, I step out from behind the counter, happy to have something to talk about to distract from the crazy feelings I've having about a man I just met. Well, technically, we haven't met yet as I don't even know his name, but it feels like I've known him for years. His kind eyes and warm smile are so familiar, even though I know for a fact I've never seen him before in my life. It's like my soul recognizes something in him that I can't help but feel drawn to.

"Oh, we're an artisan collective," I tell him. After clocking his furrowed brow, I go into a bit more detail. "We act as a storefront for various artisans in the area. We also sell some pieces of furniture, some new and some refurbished to be like new."

He nods slowly, glancing around the shop once more before settling his eyes back on me. "And that's profitable?"

My eyes raise, slightly taken aback by the question. It's not out of line, but not something most people ask. That must show on my expression because the man quickly raises his hands. "I'm sorry, I didn't mean to pry. I work in business consulting, so I was just curious."

His words shake me out of my stupor and for some reason, I feel strongly compelled to put his mind at ease and let him know I'm not offended. "Oh, don't worry about it," I tell him, lightly touching his arm. Even through his sweatshirt I can feel the warmth of his body. When he looks down at it, I remove my hand quickly. *Don't be weird, Maya.* "No harm in being curious." Wandering to the side to point out some of the stools Carter made, I try to get back to the conversation when really all I want to do is touch him again. "It is profitable. Obviously, we make the most money from things we create ourselves, but we earn enough commission from the other artisans to get by. We also have an online store and do a fair amount of business through that. I won't be buying a yacht anytime soon, so I guess profitable is in the eye of the beholder."

He chuckles lightly, the low sound bringing another smile to my face. "I suppose that's true," he admits, running his thick fingers over the smooth dark finish on the wooden barstool. "This is nice."

"It is, isn't it?" I beam with pride at my brother's excellent work. "Carter creates most of the original furniture pieces as well as some of the wood décor. This is one of his." Most of the furniture is his with how much he's thrown himself into his work the last two years, but this man doesn't need to know my whole life story, as much as I am compelled to tell it to him.

"Amazing," he breathes out, still running his hand along the wood. His eyes glance up to mine, looking a little dimmer than before. "Your husband is very skilled."

I bark a laugh, and shake my head. "Um, no husband. Carter is my brother, but I will pass along the compliment." I think I see his mouth twitch in the corners with the hint of a smile at knowing I'm not married. Is it possible this man is as interested in me? "Were you interested in anything?"

"Hmm?" he asks, his eyes meeting mine again and causing my heart to skip a beat. His eyes are brighter again, as blue as the depths of the ocean and I want to drown in them.

"Were you interested in anything in the store?" I ask again, subtly inching closer to him. I'm not being very specific or obvious, but it's been quite a long time since I dated or even flirted with a guy, so I'm not exactly on top of my game here.

"Oh," he says, chuckling lightly and tucking a rogue strand of hair behind his ear. "Probably not at the moment. I'm kind of just walking around town for a bit before I get back on the road. That's the plan anyway." The tone of his voice when he talks about leaving is sad, and it matches how I feel now that I know he won't be sticking around much longer.

I nod. With the Washington State hoodie, there was a fair chance he was a tourist, so no need to get my hopes up for anything more than a polite interaction. "Well, there are a lot of really great stores in the area and tonight is the holiday lighting festival. It's pretty magical if you decide to stick around for it."

"I believe it," he says with a smile. "There's a lot about this place that seems kind of magical, honestly."

"There can be," I say wistfully, remembering that despite the sadness of my recent past, overall, my life has been amazing. "Well, thank you for browsing and I hope you find whatever you're looking for."

He nods and steps back toward the door, his movements seemingly hesitant. "Thanks. So do I," he tells me. With one final nod, he's out the door and probably out of my life for good. It's a shame too. It might seem silly, and maybe it's because my parents would talk about love at first sight, but for a moment, I seriously thought it had happened to me. There was that instant connection to him that I felt deep down in my bones. It was like my soul recognized something in his or we knew each other in a past life. With a sigh, I go back to straightening up the shop, lamenting the fact that I won't see him again, but hopeful that the kind of connection I thought I was feeling could exist for real someday.

Chapter Four
Jake

The businesses lining the main street of Starlight Lake have all been wonderful. Every proprietor greeted me with warmth and kindness, promoting other businesses to visit or telling me to attend the lighting festival. This small town must be the friendliest place I have ever been. The mountains look perfect for hiking and the lake would be great for paddle-boarding or kayaking in the summer. Maybe I'll be able to come back during the warmer months. If I do, I can try out some of the seasonal iced coffees the barista at the local roasters told me about, or attend one of the outdoor summer concerts, or even try mountain-biking for the first time. All of those things sound wonderful, but none as wonderful as being able to see the beautiful owner I met at that first store again. For the hundredth time since leaving the small artisan shop, I'm kicking myself for not getting her name. Realistically, I knew there was no point because I'm leaving and probably won't be coming back when I'll be too busy with my new job. It's not like I don't get vacation days, but my dad expects you to go above and beyond, and I've always delivered on that front. The stunning blonde shop owner has me rethinking that approach, but that's not part of the plan.

Fuck the plan, the small voice in the back of my head says once again. It's been getting louder the more I think about the woman who was instantly alluring and strangely also seemed entirely familiar to me, despite the fact I've never seen her before. Meeting her previously is something I would have remembered just like I know I'm not likely to ever forget her. Her likeness is seared into my memory and we only interacted for five minutes.

Looking at her was like looking at a piece of my past and my future at the same time. It was a little disconcerting, and I tried to dismiss it as her having "one of those faces," but I've never seen a face so beautiful before. Her eyes were so blue and piercing that when she looked at me it felt as if she was staring into my soul, seeing deep down to the real me that I'm still discovering myself. Her ivory skin, rosy lips, and long, sunflower-blonde hair looked like they belonged to a cartoon princess. Hell, I wouldn't be surprised if woodland animals flocked to her side just to be near her calming, magical presence.

Magical. There's that word again. I can't seem to stop using it, but I have no other way of describing just how otherworldly this whole afternoon has felt. The fact that I'm still walking around downtown despite most of the businesses having closed over an hour ago is testament to just how different today is. I should be back on the road by now, back in Denver. It's only a three-hour drive from here, yet I can't bring myself to leave. If I were a believer in the supernatural, I would think I've been charmed somehow. My mind knows I should go, but my feet keep me moving toward the town square. Holiday lights aren't something that have interested me since I was a kid, but for some reason, I keep thinking that I have to see them. Not want to, but *have* to.

The small area that makes up the town square is packed with people. It's dimly lit by ambient light from some nearby stores as well as streetlamps that look straight out of a depiction of Dickensian England. I half expect to run into a lamplighter as I make my way through the crowd, but all I see are happy families and couples gathered around enjoying the jubilant music and atmosphere. Everyone looks to be having the time of their life, and even though I'm alone, I find myself smiling along with them.

As I approach the center of the square, the crowd thins slightly and I see a large water fountain. Stacks of brick surround a pool of constantly running water, a rock formation sits in the center and is topped by a copper sculpture of two doves in flight. As I step closer to the water and stare into the reflective liquid, I catch a small glare of the loose change that sits at the bottom.

"It's a wishing fountain, you know," a raspy voice says next to me. When I turn, I find a kind-looking older woman smiling at me, her eyes crinkling in the corner and a few gray hairs coming out from under her wool cap. "Make a wish, toss in a coin, and whatever you ask for will come true."

Of course the magical town has a magic fountain. "Thanks, but even if I believed that was true, I don't have any change," I tell her. With a polite smile, I turn to leave, but stop when I see her pull her hand out of her pocket and offer me the shiny copper penny that's face up in her weathered palm. "Oh, I appreciate it, but…" I never finish my thought. For some reason, I find myself picking the coin up from her palm and offering her a warm smile. "Thank you."

"Making a good wish is thanks enough," she says, nodding before she disappears into the crowd of people.

My eyes move from the retreating form of the old woman down to the penny in my hand. I pick it up and rub my thumb and forefinger over the cold metal a few times, trying to think of a good wish. "This is so silly." The words are nothing but a mumble under my breath, but I can't bring myself to pocket the coin or just toss it in without making a wish first. I've built my life on embracing routine and rejecting spontaneity, but right now, I want something different for myself, even if it may not last. Everything up until now has been routine, even a little humdrum, but maybe I can change that. With one last deep breath, I close my eyes and cast my wish. *I want something extraordinary to happen.* A smile pulls at my cheeks as I open my eyes, tossing the coin into the water and watching it disappear into the bubbling depths. The wish I just made was probably in vain, but even the idea that it could one day come true keeps the smile on my face.

The smell of warm chocolate and sugar draws me to a group of tables at the side of the square, and as I get closer, I can see a group of men and women handing out cups of hot chocolate and napkins filled with frosted sugar cookies. Now that the sun is down, the air has more of a bite to it and my hoodie isn't doing much to keep the chill out, so a warm beverage sounds like just the ticket. As I approach the front of the line, the smile on my face widens when I get a look at one of the many people standing behind the tables. She's changed her outfit, but there's no mistaking the woman from the shop I first visited. Her eyes are bright as she smiles and chats with a small family, handing cookies to the children and hot chocolate to the adults.

While she's otherwise occupied, I take a moment to get another look at the woman who has dominated my thoughts all evening long. Her hair is down, showcasing the light-colored tresses that fall to her chest in loose waves, her cheeks are rosy from the cold, and her lips are red and full. The sweater dress she's wearing is only slightly hidden behind a thick scarf and cuts off above the knee. Her ankle boots go to just below, so I only get a small glimpse of skin, but what I can see is slender and fair. To say she's wildly attractive is not an exaggeration, and I wonder how such a beautiful creature isn't married already. Of course, she could have a boyfriend, but when I look over and see her eyes catching mine, the widening smile on her face and interested expression tell me she's single.

"Well, well, well," she says, her eyes dancing with amusement. The melodic tone of her voices soothes any nerves I might have felt, and I long to hear more of it. "It seems you stuck around for the festival after all."

My cheeks pull tight as my smile takes over my face. "My plans changed," I tell her with a shrug of my shoulder, as if it weren't the first time that has ever happened in my life. My eyes roam over the rows of cups and cookies, looking for some signage for pricing. "So, are the treats for anyone, or is there something special I don't know about?"

A shadow of sadness crosses over her face, but it's there and gone so quickly I can't be sure I didn't imagine it. "Oh, well, they are for anyone who wants some," she tells me. Her slender hand reaches out and offers up a cup of hot chocolate and a reindeer-shaped cookie which I take immediately. Our fingers brush slightly as I do, and a warm, tingling sensation travels up my hand, spreading throughout my entire body. It feels as though I am being wrapped in the most comforting hug, and we're barely touching. "They're free as an incentive for people to not drink alcohol." She nods to the Mothers Against Drunk Driving banner and I nod in understanding.

"That's a great idea," I say, blowing over the top of the cup to cool the liquid down a bit. "I can't imagine wanting to drink anything other than a hot beverage in this weather, but I could be in the minority."

The woman chuckles lightly and shakes her head. "Then I'm in the minority too because I feel exactly the same. Nothing beats hot chocolate on a cold day, except maybe mulled cider at Christmas," she confesses. She turns away momentarily, smiling wistfully as she hands a cookie over to some people next to me. When she's facing me again, her teeth are biting into her lower lip, and I try not to think about how much I want to free that lip with my thumb before kissing the sting away. That thought almost has me rearing back. I'm never this instantly attracted to someone. "Can I ask you a question?" Her voice is musical and a welcome break from my own thoughts.

I lean in closer to hear over the din, but it's also a great excuse to get near her. She follows my lead and our heads are close enough that her warm cinnamon-apple smell wafts toward me. It's comforting in a way I didn't know a smell ever could be. It smells like home, only no home I have ever had smelled like apple pie. "Go for it," I tell her before I completely lose my mind and run my nose along her throat just to get another hit.

She narrows her eyes at me for a second before blowing out a breath. "What's your name?"

My head tilts back slightly, but only just. I don't want to be any further from her than I have to. "My name?"

Her head bobs, the golden curtain of her hair moving slightly as it does. "Yeah. This is the second time we've run into each other today, and I feel silly not knowing your name. I also don't like thinking of you as simply 'that guy' in my head," she admits. The fact that she thinks of me at all has a fluttery feeling erupting in my chest, and I feel almost giddy at the foreign sensation.

Pulling myself together, I try to come off a little less crazy than I'm feeling. "Jake," I tell her extending my hand for a shake. "And you are?"

"Maya," she tells me, her warm hand slipping into mine. It sends another wave of tingles through me and everything in my body is telling me to hold onto this woman and never let her go. "It's nice to meet you, Jake."

"Likewise." The grip I have on her hand never lightens, and I know enough time has passed that I should probably let it go, but I can't seem to find the will to do so. There's not much time left before I must start my drive, but I want whatever time I have left to be spent with Maya. "Say, Maya. How long are you needed here?"

Her eyes sparkle and she smiles coyly. "I can be done right now. That is, if I have a good enough reason to leave." My brain is already spinning up a million reasons to give her until she decides one is acceptable enough to leave with me.

My eyes flick to the band playing in the center of the square. "Would dancing with me be a good enough reason?" I'm not a big dancer, never have been, but I find that I'm doing all sorts of things outside my comfort zone today. The smile pulling across Maya's face in response to my question tells me they've all been worth it.

"More than good enough," she confesses. Leaning over to speak to another volunteer for a second, she finishes and steps out from behind the table.

I slam my hot chocolate, ignoring the slight burn as the rich liquid travels down my throat. After tossing the cup and pocketing the cookie, I lead her by the hand to where people are dancing. The band switches to a slower Christmas song I don't recognize, and I spin Maya around before pulling her into my arms. Her free hand slides up and grips my shoulder while mine rests at her lower back, keeping her as close as possible while still being appropriate for public. As we sway to the light melody, our eyes meet and we stare at one another longingly and let the magic of the evening take over. The world seems to disappear around us. Maya smiles serenely before resting her head on my shoulder, my cheek brushing against the top of her head as I lean mine down to rest on hers. We're a perfect fit.

As we rock back and forth, I try to memorize everything about the marvelous creature next to me. The way she looks, smells, sounds. All those things are committed to memory for me to pull out and reexamine when I get back to my routine. My heart already aches at the thought of leaving her, but no one uproots their life for one person after a small exchange of words and one dance. Something about Maya has me feeling like all my plans, all my little routines were just a way to lead me to her, but how can that be possible? It's too good to be true, but I'll be damned if I don't embrace this while I have it.

The music stops, but we don't part from one another. We stay close, our bodies practically merging as we listen to the mayor of the town introduce herself and start the countdown to the lights being turned on. Being with her like this feels like the most natural thing in the world. When the shouting of the crowd gets to one and the lights turn on, Maya looks up at me with the most beautiful expression that I can't not kiss her. Leaning my head down toward hers, I pause only for a moment to give her time to back away if it's not what she needs. Instead of doing that, she surprises me by wrapping both arms around my back and leaning up on her tiptoes until her lips meet mine.

It doesn't take any time for my mind or body to react, and the next thing I know my hands are cupping her face as I lick her bottom lip and dive into her mouth. She opens for me readily, and we explore each other. Our lips are in sync with one another, and our tongues glide against one another in a dance not unlike the one we just shared. It's slow and sensual with the promise of more, and my heart longs to do nothing but this for the rest of my life. When the band starts playing again, we break apart, our mouths only inches from each other's, our breath mingling together visibly in the cold night air.

Maya's eyes search mine for a moment, and then she smiles, gripping my hand and interlacing our fingers together. "That was…"

"It was," I agree. There are no words to describe the feelings I'm having, but they are more potent than anything I've ever felt. It's like there's a helium balloon in my chest and if she doesn't keep a hold on me, I just might fly away. My phone buzzes in my pocket, probably a call from my parents wondering if I got in okay, but I ignore it. Denver can wait. I'll get there eventually, but right now my sole focus is on getting as much time with this woman as I can. My eyes dart around the square, looking for a place we can go and get to know each other a little better, but all the windows are dark. I turn back to Maya. "Is there somewhere we can talk?" I ask. My voice is pleading as I hope she comes up with something. I need more of her, more than I need my next breath. "I suddenly want to know everything there is to know about you."

Maya's cheeks turn a deep shade of red, and I know it isn't from the cold. "Well, most places are closed now," she starts, biting that lower lip of hers again. "But, we can go back to my apartment if you want." Her eyes widen and her blush darkens. "To talk, that is."

A grin spreads across my face. "I'm not expecting more than that, Beautiful." The endearment came out of nowhere, but I'm not at all surprised by it. Everything about Maya has me acting like a different person, and while the feeling is scary, it's also king of amazing. My hand spreads out in front of us. "Lead the way." Maya smiles and steers us through the dispersing crowd over to the sidewalk. It's hard to make conversation with so many people around, so we just walk in comfortable silence, stealing glances at each other every now and then and smiling like a couple of kids with a crush, though this feels more like love at first sight. My heart soars at being able to spend more time with her tonight, but I can feel the heaviness waiting to set in as soon as I have to go. As we continue on our way, one thought plays on repeat inside my head as I look at the amazing woman next to me. *I wish I could keep you.*

Chapter Five
Maya

The door to the apartment I share with Carter swings open and I head in, dragging Jake in behind me. We haven't stopped holding hands since we ended our kiss, the kiss that will now live rent free in my head as the most marvelous, miraculous kiss I have ever experienced. My toes literally curled up in my boots. Who knew that was even a thing that happened outside of romance novels or movies? Apparently, it's a very real phenomena that I want to experience with Jake again and again. Even though I wished he had been around to join me earlier, I'm glad Carter is out camping because I plan on getting at least one more of those kisses before the night is over.

After dropping my keys in the small ceramic bowl on the entryway table, I turn around and smile as I pull Jake further into the room. "Do you want something to drink?" When I remember we don't keep any alcohol in the apartment, my lips find its way between my teeth. It's a bad habit from childhood I haven't been able to shake. "I don't have much, but I do have water or tea. It's probably a little late for coffee," I finish off lamely, gnawing on my bottom lip.

Jake steps forward and brushes his thumb against my mouth, stopping my worrying. "I'm good," he says, a smile on his face. "That hot chocolate was surprisingly filling."

"That's because it was hot chocolate and not hot cocoa. Cocoa is made with sugar and cocoa powder and not real chocolate which makes it less substantive," I say. I wince at how horrible I am at making conversation and flirting, especially when I'm nervous. And I *am* nervous, but not because of anything Jake has said or done. It just feels as if I shut myself down for a while, and now that I'm back in the real world, I'm still working the kinks out. It doesn't help that everything about Jake feels so special that I don't want to screw anything up. "I'm sorry." My hand drops his as I walk over to the Persian blue sofa and collapse into the soft cushions, my head resting in my hands to hide my embarrassment.

The couch dips next to me and before I know it, two hands are reaching up to pull mine away. Jake laces his left hand with my right, smiling shyly at me as he lifts them slightly. "I was kind of getting used to this," he says, his brow furrowing slightly. "And why are you sorry? I just learned something new, so it's all good."

My head tilts as I study his expression. He looks genuinely unbothered by my weird ramblings, and while he could just be that desperate for company, I somehow doubt a man as good-looking and nice as him is hurting for attention. I exhale slowly, turning my body to face him and bringing our joined hands into my lap. Jake mimics my posture so we can look directly at each other. "I guess I just feel a little silly sometimes. Like I don't know how to talk to people anymore." He nods and I figure if he's going to stick around, I may as well show a little more of my brand of awkward while I'm at it. "You're also the first person I've had over in a while, and I suppose I'm feeling a little out of practice."

"Ah," he says, leaning his shoulder against the couch. "So, you're veering from your routine too?"

I smile at his phrasing and chuckle lightly. "I guess you could say that, though I didn't mean for it to become a routine." My head shakes and I avoid his gaze. "We can talk about something else, though."

Jake tugs on my hand until I'm looking at him again. When my eyes meet his, they are warm and inviting. "Hey, I said I wanted to know everything about you," he tells me, his thumb rubbing small circles on the back of my hand. "I meant it."

"Are you sure?" The question leaves my mouth as I wonder who this unicorn of a man really is. Lately, I haven't felt like I'm anything special, but it seems that Jake does. When he nods I throw caution to the wind and let it out. "I haven't really been interacting with people outside of work since my parents died a couple of years ago. Drunk driver."

At that last bit, understanding dawns on his face and he nods. "So, it was you who came up with the hot chocolate and cookie idea." He smiles and bumps my leg with his. "It's a really good idea.

"Thanks," I breathe out. Wanting more of a connection, I rest my bent leg against his so our knees are touching. "I miss them like crazy, and without meaning to, I guess I just kind of pulled back from everything that wasn't essential, or at least I didn't think was essential at the time. Things like dating or going out with friends, especially to bars and clubs, felt unnecessary at the time." My head lolls against the back of the couch as I continue. "It's like I was still here, but not really. There was this hollow shell walking around that looked and sounded like the old Maya, but I didn't feel like her."

Jake reaches up and tucks a strand of hair behind my ear. "I'm sorry you had to go through that," he says. He brushes the backs of his fingers against my cheek in a move that is both comforting and extremely alluring. "What changed? What made you want to be more *you* again?"

"Hmm? Oh," I mumble, embarrassed that I got lost in his touch for a moment. "I don't know if it was one thing exactly, but I suppose I just started to feel more of the old me coming back every now and then. Day by day, my grief didn't feel quite as overwhelming as it had until one day I woke up and realized I would never be the same person. Losing my parents changed me in some ways, but not completely, and that didn't mean I couldn't still do the things that used to bring me the most joy." I reach up and touch the valknut around my neck. "My parents would want that."

"I'm sure they would," Jake agrees. His long fingers graze down my neck until they brush against my fingers and rest over the cool metal of my charm. "What does it mean?"

"Family," I let out shakily. Family has always been something I valued above all else and I want that feeling of family back. It's why I went out today, to be around others and feel a sense of belonging. It's also what I wished for in the fountain before I started handing out cookies. My eyes were closed tightly as I tossed my coin into the fountain, wishing more than anything I could have that warm feeling of family again.

"Family is important to you." It's a statement rather than a question, and his eyes never wander from mine as he says it. The tone of his voice is commanding, and I feel compelled to scoot even closer to him.

"Very," I admit. My eyes roam over his body, trying to find any indication of who the man under all the beauty is. "What about you? What's important to you, Jake?"

He chuckles lightly. "Well, if you had asked me that question this morning, I would have said routine, following the plan. Now, though, I'm not so sure." A wry expression appears on his face, making him even more handsome. "Today has certainly not gone according to plan, but in the most pleasant way possible."

"Well, that's a good thing, right?" I ask with a smile.

"Yes and no." His free hand rakes through his

hair, making the curls stick out slightly in a way that makes me want to smooth them out. "I mean, I'm normally a stick-to-the-plan-no-matter-what kind of guy, and not doing that can cause a little anxiety," he concedes. Both of his hands reach over and pull my legs onto his lap, squeezing my knees before resting his hand there. The move isn't one I saw coming, but I'm instantly comfortable and love the feel of his hands on my body. "But all the anxiety in the world is worth it because I got to meet you."

After that declaration, there's nothing left for me to do but kiss him. I've been dying to since we got here and his attentive listening and comfort has only made me want it more. "I'm glad your plans changed." My breath hitches as I grab the back of his neck and pull his lips down to meet mine. Our first kiss started sweet and went from there, but this one is skipping right past sweet and going straight to spicy. My hands reach into his long, chestnut locks and grip the curls while my tongue slips into his mouth to get another taste of the spicy chocolate flavor that was on him earlier. When Jake groans and moves his tongue against mine, I shift my legs and straddle him, enjoying the feel of his hands as they glide up and down my sides before resting on my hips and dragging me closer. When I grind down on the hardness in his jeans, he breaks the kiss, resting our foreheads together as we catch our breath.

"We can't" he pants out. His expression is pained even though his eyes burn with desire. "I'm leaving."

With those two words, I start to feel my heart crack in two, but I'm not going to let it stop me from being with the first man to ever set my soul on fire, to feel a deep connection that I can't explain but want to explore, even if only for a limited time. My tongue peeks out to lick my suddenly dry lips, and I swallow the lump of emotion in my throat. "I'd rather spend one night with you then live the rest of my life wondering what could have been." I want much more than one night, but if that's all I'll get then I will take it.

Jake's blue eyes meet mine, and I can see the smoldering embers of desire lighting anew. "I feel the same way," he says, leaning down and kissing me soundly once again.

We continue to hold one another, our bodies moving together as one, like they are getting reacquainted rather than exploring for the first time. Each pass of his hand over my hip, my back, or my legs leaves a trail of heat in its wake, and soon I'm so worked up I know I'll burst if I don't have him inside me soon. Breaking the kiss, I stand up and step back from Jake. His hair is mussed and his eyes are wide. The look on his face is one of confusion, but it clears the moment I hold my hand out to him. When he takes it, I pull him toward my bedroom, ignoring the warning that I'll be heartbroken tomorrow and deciding to live for tonight.

Once we're next to my bed, we lose our clothes quickly. My eyes drink in the sight of Jake's hard body, and my hands move of their own accord to smooth down his chest. The dusting of auburn hair tickles my fingers as I trail them downward until I'm gripping him in my hands, sliding my hands up and down to the sounds of his pleased groans. He bucks into my grasp a few times before he grabs my hand. "If I only have one night, I want it to last as long as possible." Kissing my palm, he holds me and lays me down on the bed before kissing me soundly once more.

Moments later, his mouth is trailing down my neck and over my chest. When he pulls one of my hard nipples into his mouth, I gasp and grip the back of his head. Everything he does feels old and familiar but new and exciting at the same time. The competing feelings coupled with the pleasure pulsing through my body gets me lightheaded, but his mouth moving south before his tongue licks up and down my wet center brings me back into my body. Every swipe brings me closer to the edge until he sucks the little bundle of nerves at the top into his mouth. My body tenses before I tip over, falling into wave after wave of gratification that crashes through my body.

As I come down, Jake grabs his wallet and slips a condom over his hard length. His eyes meet mine, and while they are almost feral with need, I can see the affection there too and know that he'll take good care of me. "Please, Jake." My hands grab for him and make contact with his warm skin just as he slides inside me. The fullness that fills me isn't just from his body coming into mine, but from a feeling of completeness I've been missing for so long. Making love to Jake has me feeling more like myself, and it's a feeling I desperately hope I can hold onto once he's gone.

"I knew we'd be a perfect fit," he says, his eyes sparkling. Jake leans down to take my mouth with his as our hips begin to move against one another to create the most amazing feeling of friction. Each crash of his body into mine brings me higher and higher. His speed increases as our hearts beat faster in time with one another, and when I feel him swell inside me, my body snaps for the second time as I find my release. Jake grunts and continues to pump into me until both of us have wrung all the pleasure we can from each other. He slips free from me and rolls to the side. After disposing of the condom, he pulls me into his body and kisses my temple. "Thank you, Maya." My only reply is a hum of satisfaction, and I cling to him, wishing I could hold onto him forever.

****

When I awake in the morning, I stretch my naked body like the cat that got the cream and smile as the memories of the night before play back in my mind. After the first time we were together, Jake and I stayed up until the early hours of the morning, talking, laughing, and making love. It felt like more than just sex. Even the fourth time we came together felt like it was as if our bodies were expressing a soul-deep need for one another. Now as my hand reaches for Jake, it's met with nothing but the feel of cold bedsheets, and a heaviness settles over me. I wasn't sure if he would stay or go after I fell asleep, but a big part of me had hoped he'd chuck his plans in the trash and stay forever. At least I got one night, a night I'll remember fondly for the rest of my life and one I'm certain has ruined me for other men. Blinking open my eyes against the midday sun, I turn and see a note on the pillow next to mine:

I wish I could keep you –J.

Picking up the note, I trail the tips of my fingers over the scrawled sentence, moisture pooling in my eyes. God, Jake. I wish I could keep you too.

****

Christmas is in a few days, and while I have been looking forward to this holiday season more than the last two, my heart is heavy because the one person I want to celebrate with isn't here. He hasn't been for the last seven weeks. Jake and I agreed to one night, and it was spectacular, but I can't help wanting more than that. It doesn't matter that it would be long distance. We could try to make it work. The feelings I got from just being near him are enough to make me question everything. I would never leave Carter in a lurch, but we could hire someone to take over my position and then I could go up to Washington. At least, I'm assuming that's where Jake is.

We spoke about a lot of things during the night we spent together, but last names and places of residence weren't one of them. We talked about our pasts and what we wanted our futures to look like, but we didn't really talk logistics. The only personal information I have is that he had turned twenty-seven about a week before we met, grew up in Denver, and spent a lot of time in Washington and Seattle. There are a lot of Jakes in Colorado and Washington, according to the web search I performed not two days after he left. It's not like social media was much help either, and I spent a fair amount of time scrolling through lists of Jakes and squinting at their tiny thumbnail photos until I finally gave up a few weeks ago.

For the most part, I've been able to let it go, chalk things up to one extraordinary night that felt like a small gift from the universe, a reward for putting myself out there again. When I went shopping the other day and realized I hadn't needed to buy tampons in a while, thoughts of that night came rushing back. We used protection every time we were together, but condoms aren't a guarantee, so I figured it was best to move away from the tampons and down to the family planning section to pick up a pregnancy test. Now, I'm staring down at the timer on my phone, watching the seconds tick away as I wait for it to beep, alerting me to whether or not my life is going to change. *Again.*

When the alarm finally beeps, I shut off the timer and reach a jittery hand over to pick up the pregnancy stick. "Well. What does it say?" my brother asks.

As soon as I got home from the store this evening,

I pulled Carter from the project he was working on and led him upstairs, telling him everything that happened from the moment Jake walked into Hodgepodge to the moment I realized I might be carrying a baby in my belly. He's been pacing around ever since, and while I hate to worry him, Carter is my best friend. I didn't tell him before because it was something special I wanted to keep for myself, but I don't want to go through this part alone.

"Maya." His voice cuts into my thoughts and I turn to look at him. Carter's anxious expression meets mine as he grips the doorframe of our shared bathroom. I can't even imagine adding another person to our small, two-bedroom apartment, but as I stare down and see the word *Pregnant* staring back at me, I better start getting real creative with space, and fast.

My throat is tight, and I can't find the words to express what's happening, so I simply hold the stick up for him to see. Carter looks at the results and his eyes widen slightly before meeting mine once again. He comes and squats in front of where I sit on the closed toilet, placing a hand my knee. "What do you want to do, Mai?"

My hand moves up to grip the charm that always hangs around my neck. Family. I've been wanting that sense of family again, even going so far as tossing a coin in the fountain and wishing for it. And just like my mom said, the magic worked, just not in the way I expected it to. The thought of a baby has me smiling more than I have in the last seven weeks. "I want to keep the baby." My voice is firm and I feel more strongly about this than I have most things in my life, but my brow furrows when I think about the cost and time involved with raising a child. Would it really be fair of me to have this baby if I can't support it? And what about Jake? I can't find him, so my baby will most likely never know their father. "Do you think I should?" I ask, my lip already raw from my worrying about it all night.

Carter plops down on the tile floor and rests his head against the wall. "I'm not going to tell you what to do, Mai," he says to me as he wipes a tired hand down his face. "What I can tell you is that if you want this baby, I will support you in any way I can. We have enough in savings to make it work. We can set up a crib in the office and small play area at the store." He looks at me wryly. "You know Sue is going to go nuts trying to babysit whenever she's in town. She loves kids as long as she can return them at the end of the day."

I bark out a watery laugh and sniffle, feeling emotional from the news and the unwavering love and support from my brother. "Thanks, Car. I love you so much." The words barely get out before a few tears fall and I'm hugging my brother tightly.

"Hey, hey," he says, rubbing his hand up and down my back. "Is this the pregnancy hormones already?"

I chuckle and give one last exaggerated sniffle for good measure, pulling a laugh from my brother. "Maybe. It's also because you are the best brother ever." I lean back and smile sadly at him. "I'm sorry I disappeared for a while." I don't need to clarify for him to know what I'm talking about. We've both been on one hell of a journey through our grief, I just wish I had kept enough of myself to help him through it like he's helping me now.

Carter shrugs a shoulder. "It's okay." He slides his body up the wall to standing and helps me to my feet. "I haven't exactly been myself either."

"Well, considering all we've been through, I think we're doing okay." We step out into the family room and my mind immediately starts picturing baby items scattered everywhere. The images bring another smile to my face and I rest my hand on my lower belly, grateful for the gift I've been given. "Thanks again, Carter." He nods and moves into the kitchen to start making dinner.

My feet shuffle over to my bedroom, taking in the space and mentally rearranging things to accommodate a crib, a changing table, and maybe a rocking chair. It will be a tight squeeze, but like my brother said, we'll make it work. I walk over to the queen-sized bed and take a seat, pulling open the drawer to my nightstand and picking up the note Jake left me, wrinkled slightly from how many times I've handled it. As I take in the words again and again, I could easily go into all the should-haves and if-onlys like *if only I had gotten his last name*, or *we should have at least exchanged numbers*, but that won't bring him back to me. All that's left to do is hope that the magic I've experienced so far works in my favor because I already have my wish for next year.

Now

Chapter Six
Jake

My heart pounds in rhythm with my feet as I jog on the treadmill in the fitness facility located in the basement of my luxury apartment complex. A woman is on the elliptical opposite me, and every now and then I'll notice her give me a once-over, smiling at me with a come-hither look. By society's standards she's attractive, and I'm sure on any other man her attentions wouldn't be squandered, but she could stroll up to me butt-ass naked and I would avert my eyes and turn the other way. It's not that I'm no longer interested in women, it's that I'm only interested in one woman: Maya. I've thought about her every day for almost three years and have even visited Hodgepodge's social media page every now and then, hoping to get a glimpse of her. Most of the pictures posted are of the goods they sell, with the occasional one of her brother with a piece of furniture he made, so I assume Maya is the one taking the pictures. It would be nice if someone else took pictures for once so I could get a glimpse of her, but that's just my selfishness talking. If I hadn't agreed to one night only like the idiot I am, I could at least be looking at her personal account if we'd agreed to stay in contact. But that wasn't the plan, and like every other time in my life, I didn't deter from what was laid out before me.

The watch on my wrist beeps and I end my run, wiping down the equipment and making my way toward the door, my head, neck, and chest covered in sweat from the exertion. I pointedly ignore the looks I get from the woman as I leave the fitness facility and punch the elevator button impatiently to make my way back upstairs. Once I'm back on the tenth floor, I make my way over to my place. This isn't the same apartment I moved into when I first came back to Denver, but I've had a good couple of years and what are large bonuses for if not to upgrade where you can?

The door to my two-bedroom apartment opens and I walk inside, toeing off my shoes and striding over to the kitchen for some water. I grab a bottle from the stainless-steel refrigerator, cracking the lid and taking a drink while I look around the immaculate space. The large windows shine and sparkle as I look out at gorgeous views of the city as well as the small river running through it. It's an amazing apartment, and I should love living here, but when my eyes wander the space, all I see is the emptiness I feel inside reflecting back at me. *Maybe I could call her*, I think for a moment, but shake my head and grab another large gulp of water, letting the cool liquid slide down my throat and diminish some of the internal heat my weight-lifting and long run caused. The clock on the wall shows ten to seven in the morning, so I finish my water, recycle the bottle, and head into my bedroom to get ready for the day, stowing away any thoughts of making big life changes.

My modern bedroom is just as impressive as the rest of the apartment with its smooth lines and gray walls offset by thick, white wooden beams. The large bed sits with only one side of the sheets rumpled. It's silly, but even though I live alone, I only sleep on the left side. Maya slept on the right that night we spent together, and that will forever be her side of the bed, even though she'll probably never even see it. Every night I spend in that bed is another night I dream about her. Sometimes I dream of a past life I'm certain we both lived, one where I am a Scottish Highlander and she's the Viking maiden washed up to shore. Days would be spent bringing her back to health, and we would slowly fall in love with one another. Other times I'm an army ranger, on leave in some Scandinavian country. We meet when I visit her bakery and after instantly falling in love, we marry and I bring her back to the States with me. Most of the time, though, we're just Jake and Maya, living in the mountains where we build a life filled with love and laughter together. All those dreams are in vain because not once have I had the courage to make them a reality.

Since that night with Maya, I've tried to move on and stick to my original plan. I went on a few dates here and there, but once you've experienced an instantaneous and deep connection with another person, making small talk over drinks just doesn't cut it anymore. There was one time I made it past drinks and onto dinner, but that was because it was a double date with Billie and she forced me to stay the whole time. She hadn't even wanted to be on the date herself, but she set it up because *"You need to stop it with this mopey shit and get back in the game."* That was our one and only double date. I think even Billie could tell I was a lost cause and decided to just let sleeping dogs lie, or in this case, let mopey dudes wallow. She's threatened to go to Starlight Lake and drag Maya back to Denver for me, but I've told her to leave it alone. She's respected that, for the most part, though a while back she admitted to following Hodgepodge on social media, but after commenting on every picture of Maya's brother, Carter, telling him to "ditch the flannels and post some thirst traps," she got blocked. She's left the subject alone ever since.

Trying to dispel thoughts of a future that will never be, I grab a quick shower and get dressed in my navy suit and white button-down. It fits like a glove, no doubt the result of it costing more than a suit has any right to, but dressing like this comes with the job. After slipping a silver watch on my wrist and oxford shoes on my feet, I grab my money clip and phone and head out the door. When I reach my stop at the parking garage, I exit and head straight over to my BMW SUV to make the short journey to Mile High Consulting. A quick walk from the parking lot leads me into the building where I get into yet another elevator to ascend to the thirty-fourth floor. The thirty-fifth is reserved for my father and his partners, and while the plan is for me to be up there too someday, for now I spend my hours in my own little corner of the business consulting universe.

The elevator chimes and when the door opens, I am immediately greeted with a cup of coffee from my assistant, Kendall. "Good morning, Mr. Mackenzie," he says in the friendly tone that is ever-present in his voice. "Your cortado." He hands the mug brimming with dark liquid over to me and we start the journey back toward my office much in the same manner we do every day, me caffeinating while Kendall gives me a rundown of the day. It's all part of the routine.

My head nodding is Kendall's signal to start talking as I sip the delicious espresso and steamed milk concoction. My morning caffeine is one of the many small luxuries I have come to count on. Without it, I slow down, and the desire to upend my life starts to creep in more and more. *Just quit, Jake. You know you want to.* The voice in my head has become louder and louder with each passing day. It's also getting a lot harder to dismiss, especially when images of Maya accompany the thought each time it occurs. Maya in her store, Maya under the holiday lights, Maya under me as our bodies move together, creating a feeling like no other in my heart and body. I could think about her all day, but luckily the sound of Kendall talking interrupts my totally not-safe-for-work thoughts.

"Today's breakfast meeting with your father has been pushed to Friday, your eleven o'clock had been moved up to nine, and your mother called and wants to do lunch with you later today or tomorrow if possible." I turn to ask him a question, but like the amazingly intuitive assistant he is, he already has an answer for me and raises his hand to stave off my inquiry. "I already checked and tomorrow will give you more time with your mother, but today will get you into that little bistro down the street that has that Wednesday special you love so much."

I huff a breath. I do eat that same special every Wednesday, but the smoked salmon and grilled vegetables is starting to get old. Much like my whole life. It doesn't take long for me to decide. "Let's do lunch tomorrow," I tell my assistant, watching his eyes raise in surprise at my changing up the routine. My now empty mug is handed off to Kendall as we head into my office, and I can finally remove my jacket and hang it up on the coatrack near the door. Taking a seat in my plush leather office chair, I pause halfway down when I hear the voice of my friend coming from the open doorway.

"Kendall," Billie purrs at my assistant. I sit in my chair, looking up just in time to see her making a pouty face in his direction. "Could you be a dear and get me a latte?"

"Wow. I'm surprised to see you in the office before noon. And don't you have your own assistant?" he sasses, giving her a knowing look. That kind of impertinence would usually be frowned upon, but Kendall is indispensable and Billie almost always has it coming.

Billie enters the office and flops into one of the two chairs across from me with a heavy sigh. "Ugh, she hates me. I'm afraid she'll spit in it." Billie clasps her hands together and gives Kendall another pleading look. "Please, Kenny-poo."

My assistant blows out a long-suffering sigh. "I'll do it if you promise never to call me Kenny-poo again," he says with a wry smile.

Billie drops her needy pretense and extends a hand. "Deal," she exclaims. The two shake hands before my assistant is off to gather her coffee order, and I just shake my head in response.

"Your assistant doesn't hate you, Billie. I think she's just tired of having to manage the party hotline," I tell her, logging onto the computer to start my day. Billie's direct line is commonly referred to as the "party hotline" since she's a client liaison and even though her job mostly ends after the client has signed with us, she's constantly getting calls to set up more events and parties. She's always been popular, and it seems that hasn't faded one bit as the years have passed.

"Whatever," she says. She sweeps the end of her high ponytail off her shoulder before picking at the French manicure on her fingernails. "It's not my fault I know how to show people a good time." She waggles her eyebrows and I roll my eyes at her, but smile nonetheless. "Speaking of … what are we doing for your birthday this weekend? I know we had to put it off a week since you had that big trip to meet a client and were quote 'too tired to do anything,' but I figured we could make up for it Saturday night. I do have some ideas that may or may not revolve around us attending the opening of a new nightclub downtown, but as I am such a generous friend, I'll leave the ultimate decision up to you since it's your big three-oh and all."

What I want more than anything is to stay at home and let the day pass without any fanfare. No celebration,

63

no other people to witness my misery, despite the fact that I'm exactly where I planned to be at thirty years old. My career is going well, I make a good amount of money and am well respected in the business community, and I've even looked at some houses, thinking maybe I could buy one in the next year or so. I'm exactly where I'm supposed to be, but I'm not the least bit happy. Why would I bother buying a house when there won't be anyone living in it but me? I'm nowhere near starting a family. *Family.* The small charm Maya wore around her neck comes to mind and I smile wistfully. A house with her and a couple of kids sounds nice right now.

"Oh, no." The words rush from Billie's mouth, and when I look at her I see a very concerned look on her pinched face. "You're thinking about her again, aren't you?"

I nod, not bothering to lie to my best friend. She would see through it anyway. "Yeah," I choke out, averting my eyes so Billie can't see just how deep the longing goes, but she sees through me.

Billie stares at me thoughtfully for a moment before leaning forward, her slender forearms resting on her knees. "I know what we're doing for your birthday," she announces. Two seconds later, she's standing up and clapping her hands gleefully as she looks at me.

"What's that?" I ask, almost afraid of what she's thinking.

A mischievous smile plays across her face. "Pack your bags, friend. We're going on a road trip."

"Billie…" I warn. You don't have to be psychic to know exactly where she's thinking about going. "We can't." *Why not? You know you want to go.* That ever-present voice is back and even more demanding than before. There is absolutely nothing holding me back except some stupid need to adhere to a plan my heart no longer cares to follow.

Her finger wags at me and she moves to the door. "We absolutely can. Besides, you have to come along. Who knows what kind of trouble I'll cause if you aren't there to rein me in?" With those ominous words, she exits, snagging her latte from my assistant before walking away.

As much as I fear what Billie would do on her own, that won't be the reason I go with her. As I spin in my chair and peer out the window, getting a stunning view of the snow-covered Rocky Mountains, I smile. I know what lies beyond the peaks, and maybe my pushy best friend is just the excuse I need to get me there. In three days, I'll be back in Starlight Lake and seeing Maya again. The thought of having her right there next to me has my body instantly thrumming with excitement. I hope the magic we experienced last time we were together isn't gone completely. If she's thought about me even a fraction as much as I've thought about her, there's no way it could be.

Chapter Seven
Maya

Rain patters on the window of our two-story home, and a smile of absolute contentment comes across my face as I snuggle in closer to my husband. Jake stirs slightly in his sleep, but doesn't wake, simply wrapping his strong arm around me and drawing me closer to his chest before returning to whatever dream has put a blissful expression on his face. Maybe he's dreaming of our life together. I know I often do. It almost seems too good to be true—this life, this family we've created together. Our little boy is still sleeping, thank goodness, so I get a few more uninterrupted minutes with the man I love. As I rest my head against Jake's chest, I thank my lucky stars that he never left that day three years ago. That he decided to throw caution to the wind and stay here with me, with us. "Mommy," a small voice calls to me, and I groan lightly. I want just a few more minutes alone with my man before our little love comes barreling in. "Mommy, Mommy."

****

"Mommy." JJ's sweet voice pulls me out of my dream and back to reality, a reality without Jake. As much as I enjoyed my dream life, my real one isn't so bad either. For one, it has this kid, the most adorable, tender-hearted little boy a mom could ask for. He's just over two, and fingers crossed, we haven't run into any "terrible two's" situations just yet. Even if they were to happen, I'm sure we'll take it all in stride. "Mommy," he says again. His small hand is patting my cheek lightly, and I stifle my smile, pretending to still be asleep. Barely peeling one eye open, I wait until my little guy looks away before popping up and tossing him on the bedsheets, tickling his ribs and blowing raspberries on his tummy until he's giggling so hard I'm almost positive he just soiled his diaper.

"Uh-oh, Mommy," he says to me. His eyes go wide and his nose scrunches up adorably. "Poo-poo."

One whiff of the pungent air around us confirms what he's telling me. "Then I guess we better get you a new diaper before breakfast because I know Caju won't want to be smelling this while he eats his breakfast." Caju is the closest my son can get to saying Carter. It's cute, and Carter doesn't mind one bit, so we all kind of refer to him as that.

My brother has been my greatest source of support over the last three years. He could have stayed wrapped up in his grief, but instead he pushed through it to be there for me. He helped me through my pregnancy, came to the hospital with me when JJ was born, and watches and plays with his nephew every chance he can get. Carter's also been there to give me a hug and provide a shoulder to cry on every time I've felt like the worst mom on the planet, thought about how much nicer and easier it would be to raise a child with another parent, or when I missed Jake too much and hated that he was missing so many precious moments with his son.

While I was pregnant with JJ, most of my time was spent getting ready for his arrival, but I also spent a good chunk of time trying to find Jake. It never amounted to much since I had nothing to go on, but I had to try. I even went so far as to look into getting a private eye to track him down, if nothing else, so that he would know he had a child out in the world, but the few I spoke to said too much time had passed and there was too little to go on. One guy said he could probably find something, but the cost was too high. As much as I wanted to dig into my savings and spend it, I knew I would need that money for my little boy. Priorities shift when you have a child, and maybe I made the wrong decision, but I try my best not to regret it. Sometimes I wonder if the connection I felt with Jake was as strong on his end as it was on mine. After all, he knows where I work and live, so if he really wanted to find me, find us, he could. Since we planned for one night, I can only assume he's sticking to that.

While Jake and I were sharing more about ourselves that night, he mentioned how much planning and routine had been a big part of his life, how important it was to him to honor commitments he made to himself and his father. At the time, I thought I understood what he talking about, but not to the extent I do now. With JJ, I need to be a little more structured or he goes bonkers. We eat around the same time each day and we have a bedtime routine, but other than that it's still a little flexible because with kids, it must be. JJ keeps me on my toes, but I wouldn't trade my little boy for anything.

"Mommy," JJ calls, bringing my attention back to the matter at hand.

"Right." My arms wrap around his little body and I pick him up, walking him over to the changing pad on top of my dresser. "Okay, little man. Let's freshen you up a bit." After thousands of diaper changes, this is old hat, so it doesn't take me too long to swap out his soiled diaper, toss it in the bin, and get him a new one. "Want to pick out your outfit for today?"

As soon as I put him down on the floor, he opens the lowest dresser-drawers and starts rifling through his clothes, pulling out a green waffle-knit shirt, green sweatpants, and a pair of green socks. For whatever reason, JJ is obsessed with the color green right now, and his wardrobe reflects that. With some help from me, we get him out of his pajamas and into his new clothes. As I'm pulling the shirt down over his head, I'm once again struck by his looks. It's fitting that I named him Jacob since he's basically a miniature copy of his father. Jacob has the same auburn curls, the same blue eyes, and the same Cupid's bow lips that Jake had. It doesn't help me miss his dad any less, but it does make me feel good that besides his first name, he has something else from his father. If only he could have more than that.

"Mommy hungee." I smile down at JJ and reach my hand out, smiling when he slips his tiny hand in mine before we walk, or toddle in his case, out of our shared bedroom and into the kitchen. As soon as JJ sees my brother, he rushes over to where Carter is standing near the stove and hugs his legs. "Caju," he exclaims. The sight warms my heart and helps fill in some of the cracks that formed after Jake left.

Carter stops stirring the eggs he's cooking, shuts off the stove, and reaches down to pick JJ up, blowing a raspberry on his cheek before setting him on his hip. "Hey there, little J. What do you say to some cheesy eggs and toast for breakfast." JJ claps my brother's cheeks and squishes them together. "I'll take that as a yes," Carter mumbles before carrying JJ over to his high chair and placing him inside. "What about you, Mai? You want some eggs and toast?"

I walk into the kitchen and start plating up my son's food and grab his sippy cup of milk from the refrigerator. "Um, sure." I put JJ's plate down on the table in front of him and ruffle his curls. Usually my meals mostly consist of my son's leftovers, but since I'll be volunteering at the lighting ceremony later, I should probably give myself more fuel than that. While Carter dishes up food for the two of us, I pour us each a mug of coffee, adding a splash of our favorite vanilla bean creamer and delivering it to the table. "So, did you want to come volunteer with me? It will be fun."

Carter looks at me deadpan from across the table as he digs into his eggs. "I don't think so," he mutters around his food before sipping his coffee. "I'm grateful you got it going and that it's maybe keeping people from getting totally shi—" He cuts himself off before he blurts out a swear word in front of JJ. "Totally plastered, and I'll still come and bring JJ after I pick him up from Sue's vacation rental, but that's about as into it as I can get right now."

"Fair enough," I say. My lips blow on my coffee before I take a gulp of the bold, slightly sweetened flavor. "I still think you should come. There will be a lot of single ladies there."

Carter snorts, almost choking on his eggs. "Yeah," he says, after coughing into his shoulder. "And most of them are at least fifty. Anyone close to my age will probably already know me and have taken a hard pass."

"Carter," I scold. I wish my brother believed he was a great a catch, as he is. Between losing our parents and him not having had the best luck with dating in the past, his confidence isn't quite where it could be. "Any woman would be lucky to have you, and you'll never know if you don't get out there."

Carter shoots me a wry look. "I'll get out there when you do," he tells me with a smirk.

I grumble at him before taking a bite of my eggs. "Touché." I haven't been on a date since Jake left, not that that was even a date. It was a strange, wonderful, marvelous night that I'll never forget. And it's not that I'm not interested in being with someone again, it's just that between work and JJ, I don't have a lot of time. Guys haven't exactly been breaking down the door to ask me out either, not that I'm interested anyway. Starlight Lake is small enough that pretty much everyone knows I'm a single mom, and it seems that might be too much for most of the single guys in town to handle.

JJ banging the cup on top of the table is basically how he signals he's done with breakfast, so I grab his plate before he can make an even bigger mess by throwing his leftovers around the room. "Okay, messy magoo. Let's go get you cleaned up," I say, picking him up out of his high chair. I grab my toast and stuff it in my mouth to eat later while he brushes his teeth. Once we're in the bathroom, I set up JJ with the tiniest toothbrush ever made and get him going with that while I finish chewing my breakfast and pick out some clothes for the day. It snowed last night, so I dress accordingly. The fleece-lined leggings hug my thighs a little tighter than they used to, but bodies change over time and that's especially true after one pushes a watermelon-sized baby out of their lemon-sized vagina. Jake being a big guy made me feel safe and protected when he was near, but during the most painful parts of my labor, I wished he had been a lot smaller because JJ was not a tiny baby.

Walking back to the bathroom, I pull my sweater over my head and peek my eyes out just in time to see JJ splashing water all over the counters and mirror. I quickly turn off the tap and pull him off his small step stool. "I think that's enough water fun for today," I tell him, grabbing a clean towel and wiping him down before mopping up the rest of the bathroom. "Now, do you think you can stay out of trouble long enough for Mommy to do her hair, or it is a pigtails kind of morning?" My son doesn't answer my question, and when I see the very concentrated look on his face, I know why.

A rumble sounds in his pants and he breathes out like he just ran a marathon. "Mommy," he says, but I pick him up and kiss his cheek before he can finish his sentence.

"I know. More poo-poo, right?" When he nods, I smile and lead him back into the bedroom for yet another diaper change. Who knew that such a small person could make so much waste? It's pigtails for me, I guess. If I even have time for that.

Hodgepodge's hours aren't long, but there's a lot to do before the store opens and I was hoping to finish the baby booties I had been crocheting. Crocheting is a hobby I took up while I was pregnant, something to take my mind off my loneliness, but it's turned out to be kind of a cool thing. Now I make baby booties and matching stuffed animals, selling them in the shop and online for anyone who's interested. They've sold a fair amount, and eventually I would love to expand to making blankets and tiny sweaters, but I haven't made enough to where I can hire a replacement at the shop and do that full time.

Once JJ is all clean, I pack up his diaper bag with everything he'll need when he's with Sue this afternoon. Aunt Sue has been a sanity saver, coming in to visit and babysitting JJ a few times a year so Carter and I can go out and grab a meal, go hiking, or watch a movie that isn't animated. She's back in town this week to visit her family and is watching JJ for a few hours so I can do some things at the store without him underfoot and volunteer with MADD again this year. Carter will bring JJ to the lighting festival later and we'll countdown to the lights and make a wish at the fountain. It will be JJ's first year tossing a coin in. Last year I was too worried he would eat the penny, so I made a wish for the two of us to have another year of health and happiness. This year, however, I think I'm going to try and get some of that town magic to bring Jake back to us somehow. I'm also hoping I can get Carter to make a wish for himself, but while he has attended the last two years for my sake, I have a feeling getting him to participate beyond that will be difficult.

"You two ready to go?" Carter asks from the open doorway.

"Caju up," JJ says to my brother. Carter dutifully picks him up and starts tickling his socked feet.

"I think this little guy needs shoes," he says, heading into the family room.

"Grab his snowsuit too, please," I shout. In a rush, I whip my hair into a couple of pigtails as quickly as I can and grab the packed diaper bag.

When I make it over to the door, JJ and Carter are ready to go, and after throwing on the rest of my clothes and shoes, so am I. With one last gulp of my now ice-cold coffee, I grab my son's hand and the three of us make our way down the back stairs of the building. The air is chilly, but not unbearable because the sun is out. I hope it's not too cold later. It won't keep people from attending the festival, but I don't like keeping JJ out in that weather too long. At the very least, we'll make sure he sees the lights. I know he probably doesn't even really grasp the significance beyond, "Hey, pretty lights," but sharing the tradition with him makes me feel closer to my parents.

As we walk, I look down at JJ and smile. The year I met Jake I wished to have a sense of family back, and I got it. My wish came true. Definitely not in the way I was expecting, but in a way that was surprisingly wonderful. Carter came back from the abyss of his grief, Sue visits more often, and I have JJ. It's just a shame that the one other person who would make that feeling complete seems forever out of reach, no matter how hard or how often my heart wishes that weren't the case.

Chapter Eight
Jake

The mountains look exactly the same as the last time I made a drive through this pass. Snow is settled on the branches of the evergreen trees and on the hard ground covering the peaks and valleys that pass by my car window, only the last time I saw them, I was heading in the other direction. The morning I left Starlight Lake and Maya was one of the worst mornings of my life. It started off extremely well. I woke up in bed with Maya's beautiful body wrapped around mine, her blonde waves cascading over my shoulder as she slumbered, and my heart was full of happiness. My eyes took in every detail of her face as I listened to the soft whooshing sound of her breathing. It took every bit of willpower I had to get out of that bed, get dressed, and write her a note that could never express all my feelings, but told her the one I was feeling most in that moment. *"I wish I could keep you,"* is what I wrote and what I wanted more than anything, or almost anything since I acted like a coward and stuck to my plans instead. *Turn around, go back, don't leave!* my heart shouted the whole drive into Denver that morning, but I ignored it and kept going, moving on as best I could. As best I could turned out to be not at all, since I've been living like "a depressed monk," as Billie describes it. It's not inaccurate, but maybe not the words I would use for myself.

"Are we there yet?" Billie asks from the seat next to me. Her fingers twist her dark-chocolate hair as she glances out the window, looking bored beyond belief even though the scenery is some of the loveliest I've ever seen.

Holding back a sigh, I answer her question.

"About ten minutes, though aren't you supposed to be the one telling me that? The driver drives and the passenger navigates. Those are the universal rules of road trips." Clearly, it's been too long since my friend did anything that didn't involve going from one club to another in her little red car.

"Um, no, they are not," Billie protests, kicking her feet up on the dash. "You've been there before and know where to go. I get to sit here, relax, and choose the music. That's my role as passenger princess."

A snort escapes my nose and I shake my head. "Yeah, I don't think I will be referring to you as that, but I see your point." I turn the dial down on the radio, frowning at her choice of satellite station. "If you're going to be the DJ, could you at least pick some decent music? You know I'm not into club music and techno."

"That's because your taste in music sucks," she says emphatically. Despite her words, she dutifully switches over to the classical station. "I can't believe you listen to this. It's so boring." Her voice is whiny, but she's known about my love of classical music since we were little, so she's just being a brat.

"Well, it's what I like." Clarinet lessons and taking orchestra in high school might not have been my idea, but it did introduce me to a lot of music I find relaxing and enjoyable. "You just don't want to admit to liking something that isn't 'trendy.'"

"That's totally untrue," Billie rebuts. Her designer clothes, boots, and purse say otherwise. Even though she may feel the need to have the best of everything she can afford, Billie isn't a snob. She's really down to earth and humble, she's just so used to playing herself up as the "flaky party girl," that she hasn't stopped to see that no one needs her to be that, especially me. Who she really is inside is more than enough. I've tried to tell her as much, but she always changes the subject. "Anyway. This weekend is about you, not me."

Just as I said, classic deflector. I'm not much better, though. Once the excitement of returning to Starlight Lake wore off and reality of how much time has passed since I was last here hit me, the nerves settled in and have sat like a rock in my gut for days. My fingers tap nervously against the steering wheel as I make the final turn toward the small town. My foot eases off the gas pedal, slowing the car. There's no one behind me, so no need to worry about causing trouble. "What if she doesn't remember me? What if she has a boyfriend?" I swallow thickly, trying to push back the panic bubbling its way out of my chest. "Oh, God. What if she's married? What if she doesn't remember me at all?" All these thoughts ran through my mind already, but I was able to push them off. Now that we're almost there, the doubts are louder and more insistent. Pulling onto the shoulder, I flick my blinker on and prepare to turn around but stop when I feel Billie's hand on my shoulder.

"J," she says, her voice steady and serious. You know things are real when Billie stops joking around. "There is no way she forgot you." She purses her lips for a minute before continuing. "There is a chance she could be with someone else, or married, but something tells me she's not. The way you talked about Maya is the way I hope someone talks about me someday. Trust me, if she felt even a tiny smidge of what you did, she's been waiting for you to come back."

My head bobs as I take a deep breath. My hands tighten on the steering wheel as I berate myself for having made her wait so long, but I'm coming back now. That must count for something. "Thanks, Billie." After one more breath, I pull back onto the road and we're on our way. "I'm glad you're here."

Billie smiles and faces the windshield. "Me too." After a short minute, Starlight Lake appears in front of us. "Holy shit," she whispers as she leans forward in her seat and takes in the town. "This place is freaking gorgeous. How have I never been here before? I thought I knew all the best spots."

I smile and exit the freeway. "You've never been here before because there's no ski resort, no hotel concierge ready to cater to your every whim, nor a twenty-four hour on-call masseur that you can make a pass at." Just because I know she's not really a spoiled party girl doesn't mean I still can't give her a hard time. It's what friends do, after all.

Billie lightly punches my arm. "Shut up, J. Partying and Pilates make my muscles tight. Besides, asking for their number is hardly the same as asking for a happy ending."

"Whatever you say." The car starts down Main Street and my eyes roam up and down the lane, taking in the fronts of the businesses and seeing what's changed. Most of the businesses look the same with a few exceptions, like a new awning here and some window art there. When I pull into a spot adjacent to Hodgepodge, I sit and hope other things have stayed the same. I hope Maya is still the same sweet, disarming woman I met and instantly fell in love with years ago. My eyes glance over to the dash and see that it's almost four o'clock. "The store closes in an hour. Maybe we should check into the cabin before going inside." Billie and I rented a small cabin near the lake to stay in overnight, though if everything goes well with Maya, maybe we'll stay up all night talking again and I won't even make it back to the room before the sun comes up.

Billie looks over and narrows her eyes. "No. This happens now," she says, pulling on her boots from where they sit on the floor of the car. "But I will do you a solid and head in first for a little recon. Does that work?"

I breathe a sigh of relief and nod. "Yes. Thank you." After my moment of panic on the highway, having someone scope things out before I make myself vulnerable is too good to pass up.

Billie gives me a small salute and exits the vehicle, sauntering over to the front door of the store and heading inside. The minutes drag by as I wait, and I'm tempted to bite my nails, a habit I kicked way back in first grade but can't help the need to pick up again. There is so much anxious energy in my body that I feel like my skeleton wants to jump out of my skin and run away in the opposite direction. Despite those feelings running through me, there are also the ones rooting me to the spot. The feeling that I made a huge mistake by leaving the first time, that I need to at least try and see where a relationship could go, and to stop letting my head lead me around with its routines and plans and start listening to my heart.

Finally, when I'm so on edge I'm thinking of just going in myself, Billie emerges and hops back into the car, shivering slightly and rubbing her hands together. "Woof, it is freezing out there," she says, settling into her seat.

I give her a minute to gather her thoughts, but when she says nothing, I get a little testy. "Well? What happened?" I practically bark at her.

Billie looks over at me and rolls her eyes. "I spoke with the brother, who, by the way, totally needs to wear clothes his own size. Those baggy flannels do nothing for him and he has total hottie potential." I roll my finger to prompt her to speed it up, and she sighs. "Anyway, I asked for Maya and he told me she wasn't there, but when I asked where she was, he started to look at me suspiciously, so I told him I'd come back tomorrow and bolted."

When I look at the clock, it shows that it's been fifteen minutes since she went in there. "It took you that long to basically get no information?" When she glares at me, I mumble an apology and her expression looks much less severe.

"It took that long because I couldn't just barge in there and start asking questions. I'm a stranger and that's kind of weird. So, I did a little browsing around the store first, and oh my God, there's some cool stuff. The furniture looks great, there's cool art on the walls, and there's even these itty-bitty baby shoes that look like llamas and bunnies and reindeer … what?"

I smile and shake my head at how excited she is about the baby clothes. "Nothing. I just didn't think you were much of a kid person."

Billie crosses her arms over her chest and sits back in her seat. "Yeah, well. What you don't know about me could fill a warehouse," she grumbles. That isn't entirely true, but I can concede that there's definitely more about my best friend than she lets even me be privy to, so I drop the subject. "What do you want to do now?"

A slow breath breezes through my lips as I look around. "Well, I could just go around town looking for her, but that seems silly." Then I remember the hot chocolate and cookies she volunteered to hand out and figure there's a good chance she'll be doing it tonight as well. When she talked about her parents, she spoke with such reverence and admiration that I can't imagine she wouldn't try to keep honoring them that way. There's a chance it was a one-time thing, but I have to try. Even then, I'm sure she'll be in the town square tonight, and while combing through hundreds of people doesn't sound like fun, it's a better idea that wandering through the streets, shouting her name. "We're going to check into the cabin, get some dinner, and go to the lighting festival tonight. She'll be there. I just know it."

"There he is. Man with a plan," Billie singsongs before buckling her seat belt again. I ignore the moniker and start driving. Once I find Maya, any plans I had in the past are out the window. The only one I'm interested in now is one that gets me a future with her.

A few hours later, we've stowed our bags at the cabin and have grabbed a bite to eat at a steakhouse downtown because Fran's Place was already closed by the time we were ready to eat, though I told Billie we had to have lunch there sometime before we leave so she can try the chicken salad. Now, we're walking toward town square, and the nervous, excited, buzzing feeling I've had all day is reaching a crescendo. When we get to the square, a strange sense of déjà vu washes over me. There's a band playing holiday music, people are milling about, speaking to one another, chasing their kids around the plaza, or waiting in line for hot chocolate and cookies. It's like I never left, only the ache of loneliness in my heart acts as a reminder that the three years since did happen.

My feet tap quickly as we move into the line for refreshments, and my nerves are up in my throat as we inch our way toward the tables of volunteers. It's so hard to be patient, but I don't want to cut in line. Plus, it gives me time to think about what I'm going to say. What words can I use to express the deep regret I have at leaving as well as the hope I have for a future now? I have to come up with something, but it seems my time has run out because we're at the front of the line. With eager eyes, I look around the group, but I don't see Maya anywhere.

"Cookie or hot chocolate?" an older woman asks

as she offers both to Billie and myself.

Billie smiles gleefully and grabs one of each. "Oooo. Yes, please, and thank you," she says to the woman as I continue to search for Maya.

When I don't see her, I frown and turn back to the woman in front of me. "Is Maya here tonight?"

The woman's eyes crinkle as she smiles, clearly someone who has felt the same magic of just being in Maya's presence. "Of course. She just took off to go find JJ. I'm sure she's around here somewhere."

"Thanks," I say quietly. My hand waves off the desserts since I suddenly feel like I'm going to lose the dinner I just ate. Heavy feet carry me away as I sit and process what the woman just told me. JJ? So Maya is with someone. I waited too long to come back, and now I've missed my chance. If only I had a time machine so I could go back and kick my own ass for leaving or prevent myself from doing it in the first place. But I don't. All I have left is a hole in my chest and a slight numbness on the tip of my nose from the cold.

"What's wrong, J?" Billie asks as she sips her hot chocolate. "Damn, that's good."

"That's because it's hot chocolate and not hot cocoa. There's a difference," I explain sadly as I walk further into the crowd. "Fuck. I can't believe she's with someone."

Billie rolls her eyes at me again. "Dude, you have no idea who this JJ person is. It could be a friend or a cousin. Hell, maybe it's a girlfriend of hers and they're just hanging out." She lightly punches my arm. "Don't give up yet."

After a couple of deep breaths to calm my nerves, I nod and decide she's right. No need to be defeatist about anything right now. Clinging onto the small bit of hope my best friend just gave me, I look around the square and come up with a plan. "Okay. Okay, yeah. You're right. I will save the theatrics until I know more."

"Good idea." Billie looks around the space with a grimace. "This would be a hell of a lot easier if I had more to go off than your description and could see in the near dark. I know it needs to be dark now to make the lights coming on a bigger deal, but can we have a little something to help me out here?"

The music stops and a woman approaches the microphone. "I think they're starting the countdown soon," I tell Billie, letting my eyes gaze at the people around me. "Let's split up and meet over by the fountain after the lights come on."

Billie sighs and tosses her empty cup in a trash can. "Okay, but if I get eaten by a bear or kidnapped by a killer lumberjack, I am totally haunting your ass," she informs me. The look on her face is serious as she turns and walks away.

As I navigate the crowd, the fountain comes into better view, and I have the brilliant idea to make a wish in order to find Maya. It's a ridiculous thought, but I am desperate and the last wish I made came true. Something extraordinary did happen. I met Maya and fell head over heels in love with her in less than twelve hours. When I get to the brick border of the fountain, I reach in my pocket and pull out a quarter. "Maybe more money means more luck," I say to myself before closing my eyes, making my wish, and tossing it into the fountain. *Please let this work,* I think as I blink my eyes back open. When I do, I look across to the other side of the water and see Maya with a sad smile on her face as she does exactly what I just did. *That was fast.* My eyes are glued to her as I watch her make her own wish. When her eyes open, she goes to turn and I react instantly. There is no way I am losing her again. Cupping my hands around my mouth, I shout her name. "Maya," I call over to her. She looks around but doesn't see me, so I do it again as I move around the side of the fountain toward her. The countdown to the lights has started, so it's hard to be heard over the crowd, but I will go hoarse from trying if it gets her to look my way.

When her eyes finally see me, they widen and she shakes her head and closes them before opening them again, like she doesn't think I'm real. A laugh bubbles out of my chest because I know the feeling. Seeing her again feels so surreal, the dream I've wanted for so long finally becoming a reality, that it's almost too good to be true. The countdown ends and the twinkle lights come on just as I reach her, causing us both to squint in the light for a moment before staring at each other again. "Maya," I breathe out, drinking in the sight of her.

"Oh my God," she whispers. We stand there for a moment, our smiles brighter than the lights above us. We say nothing and do nothing but stare, drinking in the sight of the other person we've been separated from far too long. Maya looks the same, just the tiniest bit older. She isn't wearing any makeup, not that she wore much before, but I prefer seeing her this way. I get to see all of her with nothing to block my view of her natural beauty. Words form in my brain, words that ask how she is, how she's been the last three years, and if she wants a future with me because the moment my eyes met hers again, I knew I wasn't leaving until we figured something out.

"Mommy, Mommy," I hear called out from nearby, but I ignore it in favor of staring at the woman in front of me.

Maya's expression changes from one of disbelief to one of panic, and the words I had yet to release stay bottled in my brain. "Oh, no," she breathes out. Suddenly, she turns from me and squats down just in time for a small child to run into her arms and pat her cheeks with his thickly gloved hands. "Hey, sweetheart. Did you have fun with Caju?"

"Lights, lights," the little boy says. His arms reach up into the air the moment Maya stands. After a moment, he yanks off his hood, tossing it back away from his head. "No like." When he looks over at me, a hesitant expression appears on his face.

Anything else going on around me after that doesn't register because time has seemed to stop completely. Now that he isn't hidden behind that puffy hood, I can see more of the little boy that sits comfortably in Maya's arms. He has porcelain skin dotted with a couple of freckles on the bridge of his nose, but it's the color of his eyes and hair that have my heart racing. His eyes are the same blue as mine and his head is topped with curls the same auburn shade as my own. They hang just past his ears, and I want to laugh hysterically that we even have the same damn haircut. He looks about two years old, and after some quick mental math, I confirm what I knew the moment he looked at me. I have a son.

A low whistle sounds from next to me and I glance over to see Billie, gripping another cup of hot chocolate, her eyes wide with shock. "I think it's time for those theatrics now," she says out of the side of her mouth.

When I look back over to Maya, she's biting her lower lip and holding onto her son, *our son*, protectively. "Hey, Jake," she says shakily. Her voice sounds exactly as I remember it, though now there's a hint of trepidation in her tone. Her eyes flick to her son and back to mine. "So, we should probably talk."

Yes, we probably should. Instead of saying that, I rush over to the nearest trash can and vomit.

Chapter Nine
Maya

Each time I pictured running into Jake again, which was quite often over the last three years, not once did I imagine that the first thing he would do would be to bolt over to a garbage can and toss his cookies. I suppose the reaction isn't totally out of left field, but I always thought if we saw each other again, I could introduce him to JJ slowly after explaining everything and seeing if he was even interested in being a part of our lives. Of course, that plan went out the window as soon as JJ called for me and rushed over. The moment Jake laid eyes on JJ, he knew he was his father. It was plain from the expression on his face. Understandably, he's in a bit of shock. Still, I always dreamed the moment we were reunited would be a lot more pleasant, with smiling and laughing and, well, a lot less puking.

Carter comes to my side, his eyes pulled together in concern. "Everything okay?" he asks, looking back and forth between me and Jake, who is wiping his mouth on the back of his hand and walking back over to us.

"Sure. Nothing crazy at all, except, you know, Jake is back. So there's that," I say, my voice hollow. As I watch the man I fell instantly in love with coming back over, excitement and apprehension flood into me in equal measure. Jake looks the same, only slightly older with shorter hair and a little more stubble than the last time I saw him. Instead of a faded college hoodie, he's wearing a sweater with designer jeans and a leather jacket. He's obviously successful, and while I'm happy he has done well for himself, I'm a little bitter because of just how much we've had to stretch every dollar for the longest time. *He didn't know*, I remind myself. But knowing that doesn't take away the exhaustion from the struggles we've been through.

"Shit," Carter whispers, drawing my attention over to him. His expression shifts from concern to protectiveness, and I feel him inch a little closer to me, acting like a shield for JJ and me.

When Jake is back in front of us, his face looks devoid of color, though that's better than the odd shade of green it turned just before he threw up. The woman next to him hands over her hot chocolate cup and he nods at her before taking a small sip. I hadn't really noticed her before now, too caught up in what was happening, but as I look at her, I can see she is easily one of the most beautiful women I have ever seen. Her olive skin is blemish free, her dark-brown hair falls in cascading waves, and her chocolate-brown eyes look soulful and kind. An ugly sense of jealousy rushes through me at how gorgeous she is and how easily she and Jake interact. Sharing food, standing close. I should have known a guy like him wouldn't stay single for long.

The four of us stand around awkwardly for a moment, Jake's eyes on me and JJ the entire time before finally, the woman with Jake pierces the silence. "So…" she says, drawing out the word while she rocks on her heels. "This is kind of wild, huh? I mean, wow." God, even her voice is smooth and honeyed, and I feel the stab of jealousy once more. She offers her leather-gloved hand over to shake, and I shift JJ over to my left hip and grab it. "I'm Billie."

The tightness that's been in my chest loosens slightly as I realize who the woman is. During the night we spent together, Jake spoke of his best friend and how they grew up like siblings. Still, even knowing the woman in front of me isn't with Jake necessarily, it's still hard to put that jealousy to rest. "It's nice to meet you,

Billie." I withdraw my hand and wrap it around my son. "I'm Maya, and this is JJ."

When I look over at Jake, he has a look of relief on his face. "That's JJ," he breathes out. "I thought maybe you had … gotten married or…" he trails off, shrugging a shoulder.

"No," I say, my voice thick with emotion. "Are you…" I can't even finish the words, my eyes flicking to Billie in silent question. Just because they were best friends doesn't mean they couldn't be more now, a thought that has me feeling nauseous and wanting to take my own little trip to the garbage can.

The stunning woman next to Jake sees this and snorts. "Oh, hell no. He's like my brother and he's basically been celibate since he left this place," she confesses, causing Jake to shake his head at her. "Seriously, it's been pretty dire."

"Billie," Jake warns, looking more annoyed with his friend than angry that she's divulging his secrets. The fact that he is as single as I am makes me ridiculously happy, though I am sad that he might have spent the last three years as lonely as I have. "Ignore her. I try to."

I look over at Carter to see him giving Billie a strange, almost speculating look. Before I have time to try and decode that, though, JJ shivers in my arms and I immediately feel guilty. "I'm so sorry, sweetie," I tell JJ as I replace his hood and hold him closer. My eyes move back to Jake and Billie. "I have to get him out of the cold and off to bed."

Jake nods and looks at me, a hopeful expression on his face. "Can I … can I come?" His voice wavers, but his eyes shine with desire to be with us.

As much as I want to say yes and let Jake be a part of our nighttime routine, he's still a stranger to our son and JJ won't be comfortable with him there. "I think it's best if I keep things consistent for him and we go alone," I tell him. There's a little stab of guilt in my heart at the sight of Jake's crestfallen face. We have so much to discuss, and it needs to happen sooner rather than later. There is also the fact that now that he's back, I don't want to lose him again. Reaching in my pocket, I grab one of my business cards and hand it to Jake. "My cell number is on the back of this and there's a coffee shop that's open late on the edge of town. Text me your number and I'll let you know when he's down and I can meet you."

Jake takes my card and immediately programs the number in his phone. I feel mine vibrate in my jacket pocket and the sense of uncertainty I have felt over the last few years is slightly alleviated. At least I have a way to contact him now. "I look forward to it," he says, his misty eyes looking over at our son. "Does JJ stand for something?"

My breath catches as I see his hand reach out for our little boy, but he stops and stuffs it in his pocket. He's respecting my boundaries, which I love, but I still feel bad for keeping the two of them apart. They've been apart for so long already. After pushing the feelings of loss aside, I answer his question. "It's short for Jacob Johansen."

"Jacob?" He chokes out. When I nod he smiles sadly and his eyes well up a little. "Thank you."

My own eyes start to water and I need to get out of here before I start bawling like a baby. "Uh-huh. I'll text soon," I stammer out before walking away quickly toward the apartment. It's only a few blocks so it doesn't take long, and as soon as we're inside I start to feel the weight of the evening pressing down on me. "Caju is going to start getting you ready for bed, okay, baby?" I tell my son, and one glance at my brother tells him everything he needs to know. Carter immediately whisks JJ off to start his bedtime routine so I can be alone with my feelings for a moment.

My legs are so shaky I can hardly stand on them, so I collapse against the wall and slide down to the floor, pulling my knees up to my chest and hugging them tightly as I rock back and forth. There are so many emotions running through me right now that I'm not sure I could even name them all. A sob escapes my mouth and my chest heaves slightly as I cry. I've spent the last three years making my son a priority, always pushing down my own emotions so they never showed, never negatively affecting my baby boy. Now all those feelings are exploding from the box I buried them in and my body hurts with the pain of having to experience them all at once.

Grief for the life we could have had together had Jake stayed, anger at myself for agreeing to just one night, and anger at him for sticking to the agreement courses through me. There is also sadness for my son who grew up without a father the last two years, sadness for Jake who has missed so much of our baby's life so far, and sadness for myself for having carried the burden of raising our son alone. Mixed in with all the bitter emotions are joyful ones too. I'm so, so happy he came back to us, that he can have a chance to know JJ, that JJ could have a dad. There's also excitement there, and I'm anxious to see if Jake and I still have a romantic connection, to see what new path our lives could take, and to see my baby get to know his father.

After a good ten minutes of sobbing and crying out both sad and happy tears, I wipe my eyes, blow my nose, and pull myself together. Smoothing down my sweater, I step over to the bathroom, just in time to see JJ drop his toothbrush in the little cup and hop down from his step stool. "Mommy uppy," he says, raising his arms.

I grab him immediately and hold him as closely as possible, breathing in his sweet toddler smell. A glance over at Carter shows him giving me a once-over, his expression concerned. *Thank you,* I mouth to him and he nods before heading out into the kitchen where I'm sure he'll wait to talk to me all about my emotions. No matter what I am feeling or how much I want to try and work things out with Jake, this little guy comes first. When I meet up with Jake, I need to make it perfectly clear what the boundaries are with JJ. I'm doing a lot of assuming, but the look on Jake's face when he saw our son tells me he wants a relationship with him. Jake might not want me anymore, and I can deal with that, but I would love for him to get to know our son.

"Did Carter already sing to you?" JJ smiles. Listening to my brother sing to him is one of his favorite parts of his bedtime routine. "Ready for your story then, baby boy?" JJ nods enthusiastically, wiggling in my arms until he's comfortable. Once he's settled, I tell him the same story I've told him since the day he was born. "Once upon a time, there was a princess who longed for a prince of her own..." The story proceeds as it always does with the princess meeting her prince and them creating a beautiful, sweet baby boy. But the prince always gets taken away by a dragon, leaving the princess and her baby boy all alone. After some time apart, the princess eventually finds the dragon in its cave and tricks it into giving up the prince that has been held captive. The reunite and live happily ever after together. It's the story of our life so far, and while the characters in it get a happy ending, I'm not so sure about the real-life counterparts.

JJ squirms and hops off my lap, toddling over to the bookshelf, his diaper making a crunching sound as he goes, and pulls out his favorite bedtime story. "Mommy read a-me," he says. Handing me the book, he quickly climbs into the small bed next to mine, grabs his favorite stuffed dog, and pulls the fleece blanket Aunt Sue bought him up and over his body, covering his stars-and-moons pajamas.

"One last story." Even though I'm ready to crash from the roller coaster of emotions I've been riding all evening, I can't refuse my baby. "Time to get sleepy, kiddo," I instruct as I smooth a hand over his curls. It doesn't take long to read the book about an extremely ravenous insect, and by the droopy eyes on JJ's face, he's ready to drop off any second. After singing him a short lullaby of my own and giving him a light kiss on the cheek, I turn on his night-light, white-noise machine, and head to the door and give one last look back at my little guy. "Good night, sweetheart." His soft snores are all the reply I need, so I walk out, leaving his door ajar in case he needs anything.

I expect my brother to start peppering me with questions the moment I sit down across from him at the table, but he just nods and slides me a glass of water. "You should hydrate after all that crying," he explains. Panic consumes me for a moment at thinking JJ might have heard it, but Carter is already shaking his head. "We didn't hear anything, but you looked like you were put through the wringer when you came into the bathroom, all red eyes and blotchy skin, so I figured it was bad."

"Thanks." My hands wrap around the glass before I'm gulping down as much water as possible, feeling extremely dehydrated after my marathon sob session. I place the empty glass on the table and pull out my phone, opening the text from Jake and staring at the number.

"What are you thinking, Maya?" The use of my full name belies just how seriously my brother finds this situation, but I don't have a good answer for him.

Lifting a shoulder and exhaling slowly, I look over at him. "I have no idea. Go get a cup of coffee and tell a guy I thought I was in love with, am still in love with, that I had his baby but am slightly pissed he never came back or contacted me so that he could know about it?" My head flops down to rest on my hands. "It's not fair of me to be mad, but I am."

Carter hums thoughtfully before I hear his voice. "I don't know that it isn't fair of you to be mad. Feeling abandoned is valid, and I think telling him you feel that way is good." He's telling me one thing, but his tone says another.

"But?" I prompt, knowing he has much more to say.

He smiles sadly. "But the guy had no idea you were pregnant and you have no idea what the last three years have been like for him." Carter taps his fingertips on the table and looks away for a moment before meeting my gaze again, his green eyes a little misty. "He just found out he has a kid, Mai. That's huge. And the way he looked at JJ, well, I could tell he was already falling in love with him."

I sniffle, tears threatening to fall again because that's the impression I got too. "I know," I breathe out, shaking my head to clear it and pushing my chair back. "Well, I won't find out anything else by staying here." I grab my phone, saving Jake's contact information and texting him to meet me at the coffee shop down the way. As I walk over to the entry table to grab my keys and purse, I turn back to my brother. "I'll try not to be too late."

"Hey, take as long as you need, sis." Carter walks over and gives me a big bear hug. "I've got things here. You just focus on doing what you need to do."

"Thanks, Car. You're the best." After giving him one last big squeeze to try and gather all the strength I can, I head out the door and into an uncertain future.

Living downtown means not having to drive often, but the coffee shop we're meeting at is on the edge of town and it's freezing out, so I hop in the sedan my brother and I share and head over. During the drive, my mind is whirling with possibilities of how things could go, but I try to keep everything out of my mind and not make assumptions. My fingers tap on the steering wheel anxiously as I pull into the parking lot, and when I look up and spot Jake through the window, I'm suddenly a lot more sympathetic to his reaction from earlier. My dinner threatens to make a reappearance again, but I choke it back and try to focus on how happy I am to see him. At the very least, tonight will provide some closure on a few things, and that's worth dealing with all the nerves in the world.

Chapter Ten
Jake

My knee bounces up and down as I wait at the small wooden table at Starlight Coffee and Tea, gripping my warm cup of decaf just to have something to ground me, keep me from feeling the emotions that have surfaced in the last two hours. I was so elated when I saw Maya in front of me, so incredibly happy that I was getting a second chance to at least see her, see if the connection was still there. When our son came up to her, I was shocked, yes, of course I was shocked, but I also felt an instant connection to him. JJ. My heart swells with pride at what a sweet-seeming little boy he was. I'm grateful Maya named him after me, but I'm also devastated at the fact that he doesn't have my last name. He doesn't even know who I am, and the cautious expression on his tiny face was like a punch in the gut. My hands twitched with the need to reach for him, to hold my son in my arms, but I couldn't do it. While I completely understand Maya's hesitation at not letting me join them at their place, it still hurt to not be near him, even for a little bit.

Maya's hesitation about me also had anger taking root inside me. Not at her, but at myself. How many times did I think of coming back here only to talk myself out of it? I've missed out on so much, and the pain of that stings like the worst kind of papercut, but goes so deep that I'm not sure I'll ever be able to forgive myself for being such a coward. The whole time we've been apart, I knew where Maya was, I knew her last name. I had everything I needed to come back to her, but I left her with nothing. She spent the last three years alone and it's all my fault. My eyes water again, tears threatening to fall, but I blink them back. Earlier I let myself feel all of that, the tears pouring down my cheeks, but I want to hold it together long enough to have a conversation with Maya. She's dealt with so much. I'm not going to burden her with my feelings right now.

The door to the shop opens, causing an icy breeze to sweep past me. When I look up, I see Maya searching the room, finally spotting me and approaching, her steps timid. I push my chair back and stand, reaching out for her, but pausing again. It feels like so much has happened in the last three years but also like no time has passed at all. As much as I want to pull her in my arms and apologize for not having the courage to contact her, I hold myself back. Instead, I gesture to the seat across from me. "I, um, got you a hot chocolate," I say dumbly. My hand reaches up and starts rubbing the back of my neck. "I thought it might be too late for coffee, but it might be cold now. I can get you something else—"

"Cold or not, the drink sounds wonderful," she replies. She removes the beanie from her head followed by her jacket, and I try to ignore the reaction my body has at seeing more of her, but it's difficult. She's still the same beautiful woman, only her curves are slightly more pronounced, probably the result of the pregnancy. A longing comes over me as I find myself wishing I had gotten to see her while she was round with our child. The painful fact that I missed that too is a sobering enough thought to quell any desire that had stirred at her revealing a tight sweater and jeans. "Are you going to sit?" she asks. The corner of her mouth twitches slightly before she takes a sip of the drink in front of her.

Shaking my head at myself, I sit back down and grab my mug again just so I have something to do with my hands other than reach for her. "Sorry," I mumble, not knowing where to start. Luckily, Maya seems to sense this and takes pity on me. It's more than I deserve and I'm grateful for it.

"So, do you want me to start from the beginning? Or do you want the Cliff Notes version?" she asks, a sad smile on her face.

"Everything," I confess a little loudly. The coffee shop is mostly empty, but I still don't want to draw too much attention to ourselves. "Tell me everything. Please." I want to know about every minute of every day that passed after I left. I know I won't get that much, but I want it all just the same.

Maya nods and blows a breath out from between her full lips before she starts to tell her tale. She begins with finding out she was pregnant just before Christmas, and being shocked because we used protection. Something tells me the condom from my wallet that we used first and not the ones from her nightstand are to blame. It may have not been as new as I thought since it had been a long time since I'd been with someone. Then Maya talks about her pregnancy a bit, mentioning it was uncomplicated, barring some morning sickness and back pain every now and then. When she gets to talking about JJ, her blue eyes brighten and a smile of such serene happiness comes across her face that I can't help but match it. She tells me all about his birth, how from the moment he came into the world he's been the sweetest little boy, always smiling and loving to cuddle with her or her brother. The more she talks about our son, the happier I am, knowing these bits and pieces of their lives together, but I also feel a profound sense of loss at the fact that I didn't get to be there for any of it. "Jake?" she asks, drawing my gaze up to hers. "Are you okay?"

I start to nod, but shake my head instead. "Not really," I confess, my voice raspy. Reaching across the table and grabbing her hand, I squeeze it tightly, hoping to convey just how much sorrow I feel at having left them alone for so long. "I'm so sorry, Maya. So fucking sorry. I shouldn't have … I shouldn't have left." My eyes get watery and I blink it back as best I can, but Maya placing her hand over mine and squeezing back has a rogue tear falling anyway.

Maya makes quiet shushing noises, and thinking about how she probably uses the same tactic to comfort our son when he's sad makes me want to weep like a baby. "It's okay, Jake."

My head shakes almost violently as I look at her. "It's really not. It's so far from okay it's not even on the same planet." Circumstances and poorly formed decisions may be mostly to blame for keeping us apart, but I feel like a good portion of the blame lies on my shoulders for being such a stupid ass and sticking to my plans. All that did was cause misery for me and for the person—no, the *two* people—I care about most in this world.

Maya stands and moves to the seat beside me, still holding my hands and resting them on our knees that are turned toward one another. "You're right. It's not okay," she admits, sniffling a little, her eyes misting over as she blinks. "I tried so hard to find you after you left, even before I knew I was pregnant, but I couldn't." She swallows slowly and takes a deep breath. "And part of me is really pissed with you for not coming back, because you could have found me if you wanted."

"I did want to," I protest. My body shifts, needing to be as close to her as I can, and I lace our fingers together. If she gets nothing else from our reunion, I want her to understand just how deeply I felt her absence and how badly I wanted her. "It was all I could think about. I wanted to be with you so badly."

Maya's head tilts and she sniffs, a couple of tears streaking across her cheeks. "Not badly enough," she says quietly. Her hand reaches up and she angrily swipes at the moisture on her face. Those three words from her have me feeling about three inches tall. She's right. I put my life plan ahead of actually living my life, and if it had just affected me that would be one thing, but I've disrupted three lives here, and I have no idea how I'm going to make up for it.

My throat bobs as I swallow thickly. "I messed up." My voice is as small as I feel, wanting desperately to make things right but not knowing where to start.

Maya's head shakes. "Maybe you did, but I could have done things differently too." She looks to the ceiling for a moment before meeting my eyes once again. "I could have asked you to stay, I could have asked for your number," she says before laughing humorlessly. "I could have at least gotten your last name."

I huff a breath, at least being able to right one wrong from the past. "It's Mackenzie," I tell her. I release one of her hands and wipe away another tear from under her eye with my thumb. "Jacob Alexander Mackenzie."

Maya sniffles and leans into my hand as it cups her cheek. "I was guessing it was Jacob," she says. Her big blue eyes blink up at me as her mouth pulls into a shy smile. "I'm glad I was right."

"Me too," I tell her, rubbing my thumb over the back of her hand. "Thank you for that, by the way. Naming him after me."

"Of course," she tells me, her eyes determined. "I wanted him to have something of yours." He has my first name, and if things go the way I hope they will, he'll have my last name soon enough as well. I may have royally messed things up last time, but there's no way I'm making the same mistake twice.

I smile, a new plan on how to get back what I lost already forming. "What name would you have chosen if it was a girl?" I ask to distract myself from going too far down the rabbit hole. Tonight is about reconnecting. Tomorrow can be about our future.

Maya shrugs a shoulder, chuckling lightly. "Jacoba?"

I laugh along with her, enjoying the way it has lifted the heavy veil from our conversation. "I like it," I tell her, smiling and bringing the back of her hands up to mine to kiss them.

"Jake," she whispers. As she looks at me, I can see the longing in her eyes, knowing I must have a similar look. "What are we going to do?"

I rub my hands up and down her arms, loving that she isn't shying away from my touch, but instead leaning into it. The question of our connection being there or not is answered, but that's clearly on the backburner for the moment. "I had some time to think about that when I dropped Billie off at the cabin." Maya nods and waits patiently for me to continue. "If it's okay with you, I'd like to stick around for a while. I have a lot of vacation time saved up," I explain. More than a lot, and while I'm sure my dad will pitch a fit at my changing my schedule so abruptly and without notice, I don't really care. My priority is Maya and JJ. Everything else can wait.

Maya bites her lower lip, a gesture so familiar to me it's almost like I've traveled back in time for a moment. "How long will you stay?" she asks, her expression wary. I can tell she's worried I'm going to bolt again, but nothing could be further from the truth.

"I'm staying as long as it takes for us to figure everything out," I say with conviction. "Nothing else matters."

Her eyes light up like I just gave her the biggest gift in the world when it's really the other way around. A second chance with her is a gift, a chance to know my son is a gift. I'm just doing what's right, what's in my heart. "Okay," she breathes out. She licks her lips and glances around the shop for a moment before speaking again. "Would you want to meet him tomorrow? JJ? Officially, I mean."

My heart stops and my breath catches in my throat that is now suddenly closing with all the emotions again. The thought of finally getting to meet my little boy has my heart ready to beat right out of my chest. "I would love to," I implore. The offer is unexpected but welcome, and I accept it with as much gratitude as I can muster when my emotions are all over the place.

Maya nods and stands, putting on her coat and beanie. I follow her lead, standing and getting ready to face the cold. As I walk beside her, I grab onto her hand. She stops walking and I go to drop it, thinking I've gone too far, but Maya surprises me and holds onto it steadily, looking over at me and nodding her silent approval as we leave the coffee shop. She walks over to a small, older sedan that's parked near my BMW, and I feel another little stab of guilt. How much did they have to go without because I wasn't in the picture? "There's a park JJ really loves that's right next to the library. Would you like to meet us there at ten o'clock?"

"That sounds amazing," I tell her sincerely. More time with her and my son sounds better than anything in the world, and I can't wait to make it happen. "I want as much time with the two of you as you can spare."

"We'll make that happen," she swears. With zero hesitation, Maya steps into my waiting arms for a hug. My arms wrap around her and draw her close, never wanting to let go for fear of losing something I now know I can't possibly live without. As we stand there in the cold, I get a whiff of her perfume, or shampoo, or maybe just her natural scent, and smile, my chest rumbling with held-in laughter. Maya leans back, narrowing her eyes at me. "What's so funny?"

"Nothing," I say, brushing a strand of hair from her cheek. "It's just ... you still smell just like apple pie."

She smiles and gives me one last squeeze before opening her driver-side door. "That's good to hear. Most days I smell like sweaty toddler or soiled diapers," she says, her eyes twinkling with mirth. "I'll see you tomorrow."

"See you tomorrow," I repeat. As I stand on the sidewalk and watch her drive off safely, my eyes never leave the car until the taillights disappear around a corner. As I get in my own car and drive back to the rented cabin, our parting words ring in my head. Never has the phrase, "see you tomorrow," held so much meaning, nor has it ever held as much joy and promise for the future.

Chapter Eleven
Maya

The room is still dark and JJ is sound asleep in his toddler bed, snoring softly without a care in the world. He has no idea just how much everything in his life is about to change, and I allow myself a moment to envy his blissful ignorance. Meeting up with Jake last night went well, or about as well as could have been expected under the circumstances. We got into things, probably not as deeply as we could have or will need to in order to work out all the issues between us now, but between the crying, the laughing, and the holding hands, I think we came to a pretty good starting point. Jake wants to spend as much time with us as possible, and I want that too, but I also wonder what happens when the few days he's taking off ends. Will he go back to his other life? Will he stay here? I don't want to leave Starlight Lake or my brother, but if he asks us to move to be closer to him, I think I would have to at least consider it for JJ's sake. He's already gone two years without his daddy. I don't want him to go any longer than he has to.

There is also the other elephant in the room, and that's the matter of what is going to happen between Jake and me. We're both single, and every time he touched me last night, I felt a warm, tingling sensation throughout my body. It was like coming home after a long time away, that feeling of rightness settling in my chest and taking root in my heart. Every time he gazed at me with those deep-blue eyes, I felt my old feelings for him come rushing to the surface. Not that they had very far to travel in the first place. It's not like I buried those emotions, just sort of put them on the backburner for a bit, simmering on low as I waited for him to come back to me. To *us*.

Well, he's back now and as much as I would like to explore the connection we shared, JJ comes first.

With a sigh, I roll onto my side and gaze at my little sweetheart as he dreams, hopefully of nothing but good things as he sucks his thumb and grips his stuffed dog, Mr. Buttons. I'm slightly jealous, not only of his innocence, but of his ability to sleep soundly. My night was restless to say the least. I think I dozed off for maybe an hour here or there, but other than that I've been up all night with worry. A fair bit of excitement was sprinkled in there too, but it was mostly concern. Concern for what happens next and whether things will turn out okay. Trying to keep an optimistic outlook is my goal, but it's difficult after so many years of tragedy and disappointment.

Deciding that sleep will be eluding me indefinitely, I quietly get out of bed, narrowing my eyes in a glare when I see the early hour reflected on the clock on my nightstand—as if the clock is to blame for all my fussing and lack of rest. Quietly, I shuffle over to the open doorway and leave my little boy to his sweet nighttime adventures. In the dim light coming from above the stove, I see my rolled-up yoga mat, no doubt dusty from disuse, and decide a little rush of endorphins is just the trick I need to help settle my nerves and maybe relax some of the tension in my muscles. After grabbing the mat, I unroll it and start with a few easy poses, or what used to be easy poses. Apparently, practicing yoga is like speaking a foreign language: if you don't use it, you lose it. Chasing JJ around all day is a workout, but it has nothing on me trying to move from plank position into downward-facing-dog. Not wanting to disturb JJ or my brother, I stifle a groan as the muscles in my back loosen. After another ten minutes of stretching, I plop down on the mat with a thud and decide that's enough for one day.

The door to Carter's room squeaks open and he shuffles out, one eye squinting open and closed as he looks around, scratching his stomach. When he spots me on the floor, he walks over and joins me on the ground. "Couldn't sleep?" he asks, though the answer is probably obvious from my very early-morning yoga.

"Nope," I say quietly, grimacing in the near dark. "Sorry if I woke you." Both of us had much later than usual bedtimes. As soon as I got back from meeting with Jake, I gave Carter a shortened version of events just to keep him in the loop. He's been our biggest support over the years, and I feel it's only fair to keep him up to speed. There was also the matter of my needing a sounding board, wanting to hear whether I was making smart decisions as far as my son is concerned.

Carter shakes his head and leans back on his arms, palms on the hardwood floors. "It's fine," he says around a gigantic yawn. The action contradicts his previous statement, but I'm far too tired myself to call him out on it. "I wasn't really sleeping well anyway."

My brother probably can't see it, but I frown at him. "Why not? Is something bothering you?"

He shrugs a shoulder and looks away for a moment. "Not really," he mumbles. He's trying to hide it, but I know when my brother is lying and he is definitely holding something back. Carter hasn't always tried to keep his problems to himself, but since losing our parents, it seems as though he doesn't want to burden anyone with his feelings. No matter how much I tell him that I want to know how he is feeling, he tries to keep a tight lid on things.

I grab his shoulder and shake it a little until he looks at me. My eyes have already adjusted to the dark, so I can see the somewhat pained look on his face. "Car," I say sternly. He may be the older brother, but I know when to bust out a commanding tone. When we were younger, I would use it to get him to spill the beans about school drama or his dating life. It always worked then and I'm not above using it now.

His head tilts to the side, lips pursed. "Fine," he admits. He shoots me a withering look while moving his arms forward to rest on his crossed legs. "I'm happy that Jake came back, truly. I want JJ to know his dad and I want you to be happy." I give him time to gather his thoughts and wait as he takes a deep breath. "It's just … I'm a little worried that you guys are going to leave. I know it's super selfish of me, but I don't want you to go anywhere."

My head nods. "You don't want to be alone?" He doesn't have the courage to say it out loud, but he nods his head in confirmation. My heart pinches at the thought of having to leave my brother and I know he's feeling the same, so I scoot closer to him and knock his shoulder with mine to reassure him. "We're not going anywhere."

Carter scoffs and even in the low light of the family room I can see the wry expression on his face. "Come on, Mai. I know you'll do anything to make sure JJ has a good relationship with his dad, and I want that too," he tells me emphatically. "I guess I'm just a little worried about what life will look like after you guys are gone."

I swallow thickly to push down the emotions that threaten to rise. Honestly, I worry a little about what would become of my brother if we left too. Not because I think he'd do something to harm himself or anything close to that, but he has a hard time letting people in, even more so after our parents died. He could easily become a recluse, focusing only on his work, and losing himself to loneliness. "Well, we aren't gone yet," I tell him, a sad smile on my face. "There could be a chance

Jake doesn't want to have anything to do with us. Or me at least." That thought makes my chest clench, and I rub at my sternum, trying to get it to subside. Shaking my head to try to banish the thought from my mind completely doesn't work either. It's still there in the back, wriggling further down into my brain and making itself right at home among my other neuroses.

Carter scoffs again. "Please. That man was looking at you like you single-handedly created everything good and magical in this world. There's no way he is leaving without you." He exhales slowly. "And I only observed for a moment, but I could tell he was already falling in love with Little J. Not that it's hard to do. The kid is too damn sweet for this world, I swear."

I smile despite my earlier misgivings. I'm not sure what my brother said about Jake and me is accurate, but he's right about JJ. Jake had nothing but love and affection in his gaze for our little boy when he looked at him and again as I told Jake all about him last night during our meet-up. "Well, I'm not at all concerned about myself now, but I am glad to hear you think he's taken with JJ. He is a very sweet boy."

"Just like his mama," Carter says, bumping my shoulder. He squints at the clock and sighs. "Damn. Only five in the morning." He stands with a low groan and offers me his hand, which I gratefully accept and am up on my feet in no time. "I'm going to get the coffee going. It's going to be a long day."

"It is," I agree, walking with him over to the kitchen. It's going to be a long, stressful, but possibly wonderful day, and I couldn't be less ready for it if I tried. The stress of it is eating away at me. Hopefully I'll feel better once we're all together. It's something I've always wanted, but now that it's here, I can't help feeling like another shoe is going to drop.

Chapter Twelve
Jake

My eyes are tired and dry from lack of sleep, my back is sore from the less-than-stellar pull-out sofa in the cabin, and my mind feels like it's trying to run through mud despite my already having had two cups of coffee this morning. Even with all that going on, my heart is full of joy, and I am beyond excited to meet my little boy today. Yes, I saw him last night, but that was all too brief and I didn't get to interact with him beyond us having a silent staring contest. I was cataloging his features, the reality hitting me that I have a child, and him looking at me like a science experiment gone awry.

Maya texted earlier to let me know he's a little leery of strangers, so that helped explain some of it, but it still sucks to have your kid look at you without a hint of recognition or desire to know you. *He's two*, I remind myself, trying to cut the poor kid and myself some slack. After spending a good half hour filling Billie in on everything, the rest of my night was spent in a fitful sleep, alternating between berating myself for not coming back sooner and the other trying to make plans. Plans that will include Maya and JJ.

Those plans are still a bit up in the air since I'm not sure where Maya's head is with all of this, and there are a few logistical problems I'll need to solve first, but hopefully we'll be able to get on the same page before I head back to Denver for work. The word "work" has me remembering the conversation I had with my father this morning after dropping Billie off at the small airport in town where she had her dad send a private plane to come get her. Even I have to shake my head at that. I may have a good chunk saved up and more in investments, but I don't have that kind of stupid money to throw around like the Kochevs do, not that they didn't earn it. I know Billie's dad worked hard in Bulgaria before coming to the US and partnering with my dad, but still. My dad isn't quite as showy with his money as Billie's dad is, preferring to squirrel most of it away for a rainy day that hasn't come yet. From his tone on the phone earlier, however, he thinks that day is today.

"You're taking a vacation now?" he asked, his tone incredulous. My father never met a vacation day he didn't think would be better spent in the office, a sentiment I shared for far too long. "The accounts need tending to, Jacob. A vacation wasn't in the plan."

"Plans change," I informed him. My voice tried for casual, but that only irritated him further. I may not have ditched my ability to plan completely, but after seeing how badly my blind adherence to them has messed things up for people who are important to me, I see that flexibility is also a necessary trait.

"Well, they shouldn't," he insisted. "At least without due cause. Tell me again what is so important that you must take two weeks off."

"I already told you, Dad. I will tell you when I'm ready, and that isn't right now," I had said with a heavy sigh. Just once I wish he could let me do what I wanted without giving me the third degree, but until today, I had always marched to the beat of a drum he understood. My veering off path has probably thrown him as much as it has me. While I don't want to tell him about JJ until I know more myself, I still want to ease his mind a little. "Just know that it is extremely important and will enrich all of our lives." My life has already felt brighter since finding out I have a son, and while my parents weren't exactly all cuddles and warm smiles, they did a good job. I'm sure they'll take to being grandparents better than expected.

"Fine," he said, voice clipped. "Just be sure to send the necessary emails to your team and Human Resources."

"Already done." I did it at two o'clock in the morning as I drank warm milk, willing my body to sleep so I wasn't a complete zombie for today. If JJ is a little reticent to meet a stranger, my looking and acting like the walking dead certainly won't help make him more comfortable.

"Very good. See you in two weeks," he commanded before ending the call.

While the conversation could have gone better, it wasn't as horrible as it could have been. My father isn't known for his flexibility, so I'm lucky he let me off as easy as he did. I may be a thirty-year-old grown-ass man, but there's something about him being my dad and the authoritative tone he always uses that has me retreating like I'm a kid again. With a shake of my head, I try to push that conversation aside and focus on where I'm headed.

After another few minutes of driving, the library comes into view. It's an older brown brick building with some metal sculptures out front, but I pass it and steer into a spot in front of the small park that sits adjacent to it. I give myself one last look in the rearview, trying unsuccessfully to tame the red curls on my head and straightening my green sweater, grateful I packed it. In Maya's text, she also mentioned that JJ is a little obsessed with the color green right now, so I dressed in as much green as I could, hoping to use anything to my advantage.

With a deep breath, I exit the car, the chilly air heightening my anxiety slightly as I make my way over to the playground. My steps falter slightly when I catch sight of Maya and JJ seated on a park bench, both bundled up in winter gear, JJ's all green of course. Maya must have heard my boots catch on the cement because her head turns toward me, her blue eyes lighting up with relief and a hint of excitement. God, I want to kiss her again so badly, but as my eyes drift down to the little boy snuggled in her lap, I remember why I'm here and push that desire aside. *For now.*

Maya helps JJ to the ground and grabs hold of his hand, walking him over to me. When she gets in front of me, I open my arms for a hug and she immediately steps inside, leaning her head on my chest and wrapping her free arm around me. "Hey, Beautiful," I murmur against her soft hair. That's what she is and what she will always be to me—beautiful, both inside and out.

"Hey," she whispers back. When I release her, she crouches down to JJ's height and I follow, trying to make myself seem as small as possible so I don't scare him away. "Hey, sweetie, this is my friend, Jake. Jake, this is JJ." Her use of the word "friend" as well as my first name stings a bit. "Daddy" would have been my preference, but I get why she did it. Maya has no idea if I'm sticking around for the long haul, though I hope to make that a lot clearer as the days go by.

As an only child with few cousins, I haven't been around kids much, so I'm not sure what the protocol is. "Nice to meet you, JJ." I extend a hand, Maya's mouth twitching at the sight before I shrug a shoulder as JJ stares at my hand like it might bite him. "It's okay," I tell him, pulling my hand back. I'm not going to force my attentions on him, but it guts me that he seems afraid of me. "I'm sure we'll get to know one another a lot better soon."

"Me too." Maya smiles at me sadly. Her eyes dim slightly before she turns to address our son. "So, little man. What do you want to do on the playground first?"

JJ hold his arms up in the air. "Mommy swing," he requests in his sweet voice. It's still hard to believe that this affectionate little bundle is half mine. There's no doubt he gets his looks from me, but it seems he got a heaping helping of kindness and light from his mother.

Maya stands and picks him up, taking him over to a row of swings that look a lot like rubber sumo diapers, and slips him into one. "Here you go, baby," she tells him. After making sure his hands are firmly gripping the chains, she takes up a spot behind him. "Do you want to do normal or rocket launcher?"

My brow furrows in confusion at the question, but understanding dawns after JJ says, "Rocket." With exaggerated motions, Maya pretends to gear up to boost him into outer space, calling out a countdown to launch as she pulls him back before releasing her hold on the swing. I step to the side to observe the two, enjoying it as much as possible, considering I wish I were participating myself. In my head and heart, I know that will come with time, so instead of dwelling on those feelings, I try to stay in the moment with the two of them. As she pushes him, Maya even makes rocket ship noises and laser sounds that bring a smile to my face. She's obviously a great mom, fun and attentive, not that I expected she'd be anything else.

Maya spies me out of the corner of her eye and waves me over. When I get next to her, she leans over to me and my body automatically follows, like one magnet drawn to another. She continues to push JJ on the swing, but flicks her gaze to me. "Pretend to be some asteroids or something and crash into him," she instructs quietly.

I pull back, raising a brow at her. If I didn't feel out of my element before, I do now. Having no idea what she's talking about, I ask the only possible question. "What?"

Maya chuckles lightly, smiling patiently as she gives JJ another push. "If you pretend like he's kicked you in the face or chest, he'll laugh." At my incredulous look, she laughs louder. "Trust me. All kids love laughing at adults in pain. It's just funny to them."

"Okay," I say dubiously, drawing out the word as I round to the front of the swing. *You can do this, Jake, you can be fun.* The mental pep talk helps me gather some courage to be okay acting like a total fool, and the fact that it's all for JJ helps immensely.

"Oh, no, JJ. Here comes an asteroid field," Maya says, nodding to me to get in front of the swing.

Moving in front of him on an upswing, I pretend to get hit in the head by his small shoe and wince with false pain. "You got me," I say. My body spins around wildly and I clutch my eye with one hand as I rub at my forehead with the other, acting like it really hurts.

The sounds of my little boy giggling has my heart filling up with so much happiness I feel like it might burst. Needing to hear that sound again like I need my next breath, I push aside any instinct to maintain any sense of composure and repeat the action, earning an even bigger giggle from my boy and a smile from his mom. "Again," JJ shouts happily. He claps his hands as he swings and I smile at the expression of pure joy on his face.

"You got it," I tell him. Over and over, I pretend to get hit in the face, in the shoulder, even going so far as pretending to fall down completely, causing a giggle fit so delightful I almost wish I had stopped to get a recording of it so I could play it back. JJ's laughter is a medicine I didn't know I needed. It's a balm to my soul, slowly helping to seal up the cracks in my heart that splintered the moment I realized he was mine and I hadn't been there for him.

"All right, little man." Maya grabs the chains and gradually slows the swing to a stop. "Let's give the asteroids a break from all that pummeling." She picks him up out of the swing and sets him down on the wood chips scattered around the playground. "Want to go climb to the top of the tower?"

"Tower," he shouts happily. Running forward, he grabs my hand. I'm awestruck and so focused on the feel of his soft tiny hand in mine that I don't move right away. JJ tugs on my fingers. "Tower," he commands again. With I'm sure is a dopey grin on my face, I follow along as he pulls me over to the large structure on the other side of the playground.

As I glance back at Maya, she has a wide grin on her face, but her eyes are a bit misty. "Have fun, you two." She steps over to the ladder with us but refrains from climbing up. "I'll stay down here and keep watch for space aliens who want to try and take over your fortress."

"Okay, Mommy." JJ grabs the bottom rung and I automatically brace my hands next to him to catch him should he fall. As I do, I realize that even after such a short time together, I'm already so completely attached to this kid that I want to always be there to catch him, no matter what. He's mine and I'm his, and even though the path ahead may be a little rocky and unclear, anything I must do to be with him and Maya will be worth it.

After a full ninety minutes of playing both as a threesome and just the two of us, it seems JJ is ready for lunch. By the smell of things, a possible diaper change may be in order as well. "I can run into the library to change his diaper and then we can head over to Fran's Place for lunch if you like." Maya bites her lower lip as she holds onto JJ. "Or, if you'd rather not…"

I still her worrying with a hand on her shoulder.

"Maya." My eyes bore into hers, trying to convey just how much I want to be there with the two of them, now and as often as she'll allow it. "I meant what I said last night. I want as much time with the two of you as I can get."

She sighs, looking relieved and pleased. "Okay." She starts walking toward the library entrance and smiles at me. "I had fun this morning," she confesses, smiling shyly for a moment before facing forward. "It was nice, having you there with us, and not just because I got a break from running around or getting wood chips thrown in my hair."

A chuckle breaks loose from my chest and I smile at the mental picture she paints of how their park dates normally go. "It was nice being able to be there with the two of you," I tell her. My steps halt, stopping our progress on the flagstone path for a moment. "I'd like there to be a lot more of this, if you're willing."

"Of course I am." Her voice is firm and full of certainty as she cuddles our little boy tighter as his tired head lolls on her shoulder. "I want that for him."

I brush the back of my knuckles against her smooth cheek as I gaze into her sky-blue eyes. "Just him?"

She shivers and I smile, knowing it isn't from the cold. "No, not just for him," she admits quietly. She stays smiling at me for a moment before her face turns serious again. "But he still comes first. I need you to understand that, Jake. What you or I want doesn't really matter as much as what he needs or what's best for him." Her blue eyes search mine as I process what she's just told me. "Does that make sense?"

My head bobs in understanding where she's coming from. The fact that she's probably spent the last three years sacrificing so much for herself to put our son first hits me hard, and I nearly give into the anger at myself once again. Instead, I make a vow that it will never happen again. JJ comes first, but Maya comes first too, at least in my book. She may not realize it yet, but she just solidified my plans. "It makes a lot of sense," I reply, cupping her face for a moment. "I'll do everything in my power to make sure he always gets what's best for him." *And for you too*, I add silently.

Maya is all smiles once again as we continue to the library. It's been less than a day, but being with the two of them already feels as natural as breathing. I just hope the plans I'm coming up with are agreeable to Maya. If she doesn't want me to stay, it will break my heart. A heart that has and always will belong to her and the little boy cradled in her arms.

Chapter Thirteen
Maya

Lunch at Fran's Place was an interesting affair. Jake and I had a great time catching up on the more mundane side of our lives over the last few years. Even though he's only two, JJ picks up on a lot more than most people would think, so we kept it light, sticking to subjects like work or JJ's likes and dislikes, habits, and routines. When the food arrived, Jake had been strangely excited about their chicken salad. Noticing my curious glance, he explained the story of the last time he came and how he had been convinced to live a little more and plan a little less that day. Well, he definitely did that, and I'm grateful for it. The result was our wonderful night together and the little boy that was so out of it during the meal that he kept yawning. About two minutes after we left the restaurant, JJ passed out in his car seat from the excitement and exhaustion of the morning.

Jake was following us back to our place, but I called him and told him I would be driving around a bit first so that JJ could sleep. Never wake a sleeping toddler, I told him, especially one that has a hard time falling asleep after even the shortest of catnaps. I fully expected Jake to go back to his rented cabin and rest, but instead he asked if I would pull over and we could drive around the town together to catch up. He mentioned being curious about the town where we live, so I did as he asked, hoping that giving him a tour of Starlight Lake might make the idea of him staying here even more appealing. The thought of asking him to uproot his life for us makes me a little nauseous, but the idea of being a real family is too tempting to push it aside completely. I'll just tuck it away for later and see how the rest of his time here goes. If it goes as well as the park and lunch did, I don't think it will take me long to work up the courage to ask.

Watching Jake and JJ play together was the most heartwarming thing I've witnessed in a while. Life with a child is full of heart-warming moments, but only a few really stick out as ones that will live in your memory for years to come. That happened today as I watched JJ slip his hand into his father's before running off to play with him. My fingers twitch with excitement, needing to write down every observation, every emotion I experienced watching my little boy bond with his daddy.

Throughout my life, I kept diaries and journals off and on, but it was never really a priority until I got pregnant. The journals I started then contain everything that happened, everything I felt, and every hope I had for the baby growing in my belly. After JJ was born, I kept it going, but instead it focused mostly on his milestones and particularly cute moments that would happen from time to time. Looking over at Jake in the passenger seat, a tranquil expression on his face as his body is twisted around so he can watch our little boy slumber, I make a mental note to give the journals to him soon. Jake's the main reason I kept them after all. If he ever came back to us, I didn't want him to feel as though he completely missed out on the last few years.

Jake must sense me watching him because he turns back to the front as I make a turn around the lake. Out of the corner of my eye, I see him looking a little apprehensive. I signal to turn toward my old neighborhood and nod my head at him. "All right, you. Out with it?"

"Out with what?" he asks. His voice goes slightly higher as he plays innocent when I am sure there is something running around in that brain of his. If his brain is anything like mine, it's been running nonstop since the moment I saw him again.

"Out with whatever has you looking like you want to roll out of this car as soon as I slow down long enough," I press on, giving him a brief but stern look.

He huffs a breath and holds up his hands. "Okay, okay," he says with a small smirk. "You can put away the mom look."

I chuckle lightly, trying to lighten the mood and because I do have a mom look now. While I don't need to use it on my son much, I have found that it has come in handy with my brother, and now Jake. Dramatically schooling my features, I look at him as blankly as possible. "There, Mom look gone."

"Thank you," he says, peeking over his shoulder at JJ one more time. "Remind me never to get on your bad side. That look could wilt lettuce." When I raise a brow, he seesaws his head. "Okay, I'll quit stalling." While I love that we're in sync enough for me to know when he is putting off telling me something, I am a little worried about what he might say. Trying to focus on the road in front of me and not the gorgeous man in the passenger seat, I give him space to gather his thoughts. The sound of a deep inhale and exhale drifts over to my ears before his deep voice finally does. "Well, I was just thinking that we made one beautiful-looking kid, but beyond that, he's also sweet and mild-tempered. You did an amazing job, Maya." His fingers tap against his leg for a moment. "He's so great ... it's almost like I wasn't really needed at all."

My foot slips off the gas for a moment because of how shocked I am to hear him say that and how heartbreaking the despondent tone of his voice is. After checking for traffic, I pull off the road in front of a row of houses and put the car in "park." Unbuckling my seat belt, I turn to face him, not liking the look of sadness in his eyes. How can he possibly think he wasn't necessary? Reaching over, I take one of his hands in both of mine, holding onto it as tightly as possible. "First, thank you for telling me that I did well with our son because most of the time I feel like I'm middling at best." I can see him going to protest this, so I hold up a hand to stop him. "No need to say otherwise. Believing in my Mom skills is something I'm already working on, so just let me keep going."

"Okay," he breathes out, shifting in the seat that's too small for his large from so that he can face me more fully. "I won't interrupt."

With a nod, I try to think of the best way to phrase exactly just how needed he was without making him feel too guilty for his absence. I'm not sure there are the right words for this, so I just continue my argument as best I can, pushing past the pain that comes whenever I think about just how hard the last three years have been. "You were needed, Jake, but beyond that, you were wanted and you were missed." I swallow thickly as the weight of the last three years presses down on me, like a boulder on my chest. "There were so many times I wanted to talk to you, to have you hold me, to have you know our son. And yes, he is amazing and we did our best, we got by, but that doesn't mean you weren't needed. You were, are, and always will be completely necessary to his life." My eyes mist over and I blink away the tears. "I just ... I don't think I can ever express just how much you being here means to me." I look back at JJ who is still sleeping peacefully despite the conversation happening in the front seat. "I know he can't show it yet, but it means a lot to him too. I can tell."

Jake places his other hand over mine and squeezes it tightly, an expression of profound gratitude on his face.

"Thank you for saying that, Beautiful." He lifts a finger to swipe away a tear that fell from my eye. "I'm glad the two of you were okay, but you won't have to just get by anymore. Not if I have anything to say about it."

I sniffle and nod, not able to speak anymore. Able to read me so well after only being back together briefly, Jake pulls me into his arms and lets me weep quietly against his shoulder for a bit. Dampness from my tears spreads across his sweater, but I can't bring myself to pull away just yet. Finally, after I've ridden the wave of emotion as far as it will go, I sniffle one last time and lean back, swiping a tissue from the console between us and wiping my nose. "I'm sorry I cried all over you," I tell him with a nod at his soaked sweater. Cleaning myself up as best I can and tossing the tissue in the trash, I take a few deep breaths to calm myself fully. "It's just been a lot to handle. I have my brother and Aunt Sue whenever she comes to visit, but it's not the same."

He smiles sadly at me. "I'm sure it isn't, and I know you're probably sick of hearing me say this, but I really am sorry." He shrugs a shoulder and glances out the windshield. "I let old habits and listening to my head get in the way of something really special." When he turns back to me, his eyes are a deep ocean blue and full of a fiery determination. "That won't be happening again. I need you to trust that. Trust me."

"I do," I tell him. With that meaningful look on his face, I would believe in just about anything he would say. And I trust him more than I trust almost anybody, which is a bit scary seeing as how he's only been back for one day. There has always been something about Jake that had me feeling safe and protected. I trust my gut and I trust him. He could easily break that trust and break my heart at any moment, but I don't think he will. "I do trust that."

Jake grips my chin with his thumb and forefinger, narrowing his eyes and inspecting my gaze as if to determine whether or not I mean what I say. When he sees that I do, he nods curtly. "Good," he breathes out. His body leans back in the seat, looking like those few words just took the weight of the world off his shoulders.

As he's leaned back, I catch a glimpse of the house outside the window, a small gasp escaping my mouth. "Oh my God. I can't believe they changed the color," I say aloud. My eyes sweep over what was once a bright yellow, cottage-style two-story building that Carter and I once called home. It's now a dull green with a brick-red trim. Driving by it has been something Carter and I have managed to avoid over the years, but apparently my idly driving around our old neighborhood led us directly in front of the old place. Seeing the changes to our old home breaks my heart, the happiness that I experienced there seemingly covered up by the new paint and other alterations. "It's so sad looking."

Jake's head whips around to look out the window. "It has zero curb appeal. I mean, look at the state of the yard," he says offhandedly. At his comment, my eyes move away from the house, and I notice that the flower beds my mother prided herself on are overgrown with dead weeds, as is the rest of the front lawn after years of neglect. When he looks back at me, I wonder if he can read the devastation on my face because he cups my jaw and steers my gaze over to his. "This is the house you guys grew up in. The one you had to sell, isn't it?" When I nod, he pulls me close again and rubs his hand soothingly up and down my back. "I'm sorry, Beautiful."

I shrug in his arms, but wrap mine around him just the same. "It's just a house." Even as I say it I know the words are a lie. That house is so much more than that. It's years of memories and happy times with my parents, it's a place where I felt completely safe and accepted as who I am, and it's a place I had hoped I would get to share with my kids someday. Now, it's no longer a home, it's just a cheerless building with a hideous yard. It makes me sad to think about all the laughter that had echoed around that house and is now probably buried under a bunch of dust and cobwebs.

"It's not just a house, but I admire you trying to be brave about it." He leans back just enough to kiss my forehead, the gesture itself along with the warmth of his lips like a soothing salve for the pain in my heart. "Just remember, they can't paint over all the wonderful memories you have up here," he says. His fingers lightly touch my temple before brushing through my hair. I tilt my head back slightly, blinking up at him, wanting him to kiss me so badly I can feel my lips tingling with the need for them to be connected to his.

"Jake," I whisper, inching my mouth closer to his. I have waited for this kiss for three years, but I can't wait any longer. Our lips barely brush before I hear our son stirring in the back seat. Instantly, I lean back, peeking over toward the back to see JJ stretching his arms and legs wide in his seat. When his eyes meet mine in the little mirror on the headrest behind him, I smile. "Hey, sweetie. Did you have a good nap?"

"Sleepy," he says quietly before yawning. My eyes flick to the dash and I see he only got about forty minutes when normally he gets at least two hours. Bedtime should be interesting tonight. "Go home?"

"Sure, baby. We can go home," I tell him. Buckling myself in again and pulling back onto the street, I flick my eyes over to Jake. His eyes are dim, and overall he's looking a little sad, and I wonder if he doesn't want this day to end either. As far as I'm concerned, this day could and should go on forever. "Would you want to come over for a bit? You could even stay for dinner if you like."

His eyes immediately brighten. "That would be great," he says, spinning in his chair and reaching back to ruffle JJ's curls. "If it's okay, do you think I could stay for bedtime too?" His eyes widen and a blush comes across his face. "JJ's bedtime, I mean. Obviously."

I nod, stifling a smile. "Oh, obviously," I tell him, unable to hide my smirk any longer. "And yes, I think if everything goes well, you can stay for bedtime. Though be warned, it can get a little hairy on car nap days." I'll be surprised if JJ is at all agreeable tonight, but maybe we'll get lucky.

"I think I'm up for the challenge," he assures me. I sure hope he means what he says. It's easy to want to stick around when your kid is all sunshine and cute smiles, but when things get rough, the desire to escape can get very, very real. Everything in my being tells me he'll stay, and I kick myself for not being more specific with my wish last night. I wished for Jake to come back to us, but I should have added one word that could make all the difference. I should have added the word "stay."

Chapter Fourteen
Jake

The apartment above Hodgepodge looks almost exactly as I remember it. The exposed brick walls and hardwood floors are the same contrasting shades of brown, the blue sofa and chairs still sit in front of the large window that is currently letting in the afternoon sun, and the kitchen is still small, but cozy, with an elegant-looking dining table sitting on the other side of the island. I would bet good money the table is one their father created. It has an older style that's different from the pieces I've viewed of Carter's. Speaking of Carter, the man is staring at me, a vaguely menacing expression on his face as he leans against the kitchen counter, arms crossed over his chest.

Seeing that he's not going to budge, I step up to him as Maya removes her and JJ's coats. "You must be Carter," I say, extending a hand. "I'm Jake. It's a pleasure to meet you."

Carter looks at my hand like I recently stuck it in the toilet or one of JJ's soiled diapers, but he grips it and gives it a shake anyway. His grip is strong, probably from all the woodworking he does, and while I can tell he's trying to intimidate me, it won't work. First, I have at least three inches on him and workout regularly, but more than that, I have only good intentions toward his sister and nephew, so there's really no reason for him to be protective, though I understand his motivation for doing so. "Nice to meet you too," Carter replies, pulling me closer. "You hurt either one of them and I will drop you so far down into the bottom of that lake out there no one will ever find you."

"Carter!" Maya's exasperated voice sounds near

us and Carter drops my hand, stepping back and looking slightly abashed. "There's no need for that."

Carter tosses his hands up. "All right," he says, looking over at me with a shrug. "Sorry, man. My dad was the Viking, not me. Doesn't mean I don't still try every now and then."

I chuckle lightly to dispel the remaining tension between us. "No worries," I tell him as I remove my own coat. "I appreciate you defending the two of them so diligently." My lightheartedness dies off as I realize that Carter is probably one of the main reasons Maya and JJ are doing as well as they are. Adopting a more serious tone, I step up and clasp the man's shoulder. "Actually, I appreciate a lot more than just that." I swallow my hurt pride at not having been able to provide for my family and take a deep breath. "Thank you for helping take such good care of Maya and JJ. It means a lot to me."

Carter blushes slightly and lifts a shoulder, clearly uncomfortable with my words. "It's not a big deal, but you're welcome."

I simply nod, not wanting to give any more unwanted attention to him than necessary. Maya mentioned Carter was a lot shier than she was, and clearly she knows what she's talking about. Stepping over to JJ, I kneel down to him and help take his shoes off. I glance over at Maya to see her smiling at us, and my breath catches again at just how strikingly beautiful she is. Her eyes that seem to see into my soul and her blonde locks that reflect the light still remind me of some otherworldly creature, someone too magical for the likes of me, yet I want her anyway. "What's on the agenda for this afternoon?" I ask. The question is an attempt to refocus on the three of us instead of trying to get some alone time with Maya. There will be plenty of time for that since I plan on sticking around for a while.

"Hmm," she says, tapping her hand on the side of her leg. "Normally Sundays are for grocery shopping, but Carter already took care of that." Her head nods gratefully at her brother. "So I guess it's really anything goes."

I turn to JJ, smiling down at his little face. "Hey, bud," I say to him, holding out my hand. "Want to show me your room?" JJ nods emphatically and grabs onto my thumb, pulling me toward the room that I remember as Maya's.

Standing, I follow along quickly as he leads me into the doorway and stops in front of a small bed with sheets covered with woodland animals. I pointedly ignore the queen-sized bed in the room, not wanting to go down a rabbit hole of memories of the time I spent in it with Maya. Those thoughts are not kid-time appropriate, so I maintain my focus on JJ as he moves around. Next to the bed is a small bookcase with books, a few stuffed toys, and a wooden block set, but not much else. "My room," he explains. His small hands reach onto the bookshelf to grab the container of wooden blocks before hauling it to the rug on the floor. "Play a-me?" he asks, and of course my answer is yes.

"I would love to play with you," I tell him sincerely. Happiness causes my heart to swell once more as I plop down on the ground in the small space between the bookshelf and Maya's bed. Grabbing a few of the blocks and starting to stack them up, I inspect each one as I do. The surface of the blocks is smooth and shiny, and as I look at the carvings on the sides, I can see that they're most likely another custom Carter creation. I'm slightly jealous that he's been able to give so much to my son when I have given so little, but I try to remind myself that I'm going to change all that. Stowing my hurt feelings for later, I turn my focus to playing with JJ.

"What should we make fist, bud? Do you want to make a castle, or should we build a fort?" They're basically the same thing, but he doesn't know that and I'm really just trying to see how many words he can use.

"Make fort," he says with a smile. He pushes more of the blocks at me. After I stack a bunch together and make my approximation of a fort, JJ reaches to the bed behind him and grabs a stuffed dog. Making small barking noises, he makes the dog hop over to the blocks and proceeds to smash the fort.

I laugh as the dog demolishes my hard work. "There goes the fort," I say through a chuckle, enjoying the look of happiness on my little boy's face.

"Again," he shouts, pushing the blocks toward me once more. One look into his deep-blue eyes has me smiling and stacking the blocks all over again.

"Uh-oh," Maya calls from the open doorway. I look over and see a wry smile on her face. "I can tell this little guy already has you wrapped around his finger."

I shrug and smile wider. "Not even going to try and deny it," I tell her. With rapt attention, I watch as she walks over to the bed and lays down on it, her body turned toward the two of us. Thank God, JJ starts demanding I keep building because I was dangerously close to fantasizing about the last time I saw Maya in that bed and how the two of us passed the time that night.

After another twenty minutes of blocks, I look over to Maya on the bed. Her eyes are closed as her head lies upon a bent arm as she naps peacefully. Realizing she probably gotten about as much rest as I did last night and knowing she's probably about three years behind on regular sleep, I hold a finger up to my mouth for JJ to be quiet and sneak him out of the room. After closing the door, I walk JJ over to the dining table where Carter is working on a laptop. "Caju," JJ exclaims happily, running over to his uncle for a hug. He climbs onto Carter's lap readily, and I squash that jealously down once more. *Eyes on the prize, Jake*, I remind myself. It's not about what I lost, but about what I've gained and what I need to do to keep it.

"Hey, Little J." Carter kisses the top of JJ's head and shuts his laptop. He looks up at me with a furrowed brow as I approach the dining table. "Where's Maya?"

I hike a thumb over my shoulder and point to her bedroom. "She fell asleep while we were playing, so I thought it best to leave her be," I explain. My mind blanks as I try to think of what JJ and I can do together now. We've played a lot today, but surely there are other things one does with a child. Maybe I should pick up a parenting book or two from the bookshop I spied on our drive after lunch. Or, I could suck it up and ask the one other person who knows my son best. He is sitting in front of me, after all. "The two of us played with his blocks already … is there some other activity he likes to do?"

"Sure," Carter says, pointing to a basket in the corner. "We set up a play area in the office downstairs for him until he starts preschool next year, so we keep most of his toys there, but there are a few items he likes. He also loves watching *Daniel Tiger* every now and then."

My brow furrows. I don't know much about kids, but I have seen articles and heard people in the office talk about kids and screen time over the years. They all say that it's a bad thing, so I'm not sure JJ watching television is what's best for him. "Does he watch a lot of television? I mean, I've heard stuff on the news about the importance of limiting screen time, so I'm not sure that's the best idea."

Carter stares at me a moment, his lips pressed together in a thin line. Finally, he nods curtly. "Oh, heard things, have you?" he asks. He moves and sets JJ down on his seat, setting him up with some paper and crayons. "Hey, Little J. Do you want to draw Mommy a picture?" JJ nods and grabs at an almost comically large green crayon and starts scribbling on the white paper. Carter smiles at JJ, but when his face turns to me, the smile drops right off his face and his expression morphs into something much less friendly. "Follow me," he commands as he steps over to the other side of the room. When he turns, his expression is not only unfriendly, it's downright hostile. "What the fuck, man?" he asks in a harsh whisper.

I shake my head, totally caught off guard by the venom I hear in his voice. "What do you mean? I was only asking a question." I'm not sure what I said that set him off, but clearly I've made some kind of misstep, at least in his eyes.

Carter crosses his arms over his chest defensively. "No, you were only implying that whatever you have heard means that the way Maya has been parenting him is subpar." He takes a deep breath and closes his eyes, pinching the bridge of his nose. "Look, Jake. I'm sure you're a good guy, and I know Maya cares a great deal about you and wants everything to work out with the three of you."

"I care about her too," I protest, feeling more solid about that than anything. "I just want to make sure JJ gets what's best for him."

Carter nods and sighs. "I get that, I do. But you haven't been here, and Maya has. Is she the perfect mom? No, because no one is," he says quietly. His eyes dart to the still closed door of her room before he continues. "But she has essentially been working two jobs while single-handedly raising him. Working the front of the store while creating items to sell to bring in extra cash.

Did you know that?" I shake my head. From what she had mentioned about the last few years, I knew they had it a little harder than most, but I had no idea Maya had been running herself ragged like that. My heart drops to my stomach with the knowledge of it. "Sue helps when she's in town, but that's like three times a year at most. I help too, but there's only so much I can do while trying to keep the business profitable enough to keep us afloat. And that's just the day-to-day stuff. There's a huge emotional burden she has carried almost entirely by herself for three years, so if she has to put on a television show to distract him for twenty minutes in order to catch the bare minimum of time for herself, so be it." He stares me dead in the eyes. "JJ's mom having a breakdown from exhaustion or stress will hurt him a hell of a lot more than a little screen time will."

Feeling sufficiently chastised, I nod and try not to let how ashamed I feel about what I just said, and how much I woefully underestimated just how tough it's been for Maya, get to me too much. When I'm alone in the cabin later, I can let myself feel all of it and work on making things right. Until then, I'll do my best to make it through the rest of the day without saying something stupid again. "Sorry," I choke out, my breathing slightly ragged. The apology is inadequate, but I don't trust my voice not to waver if I say more.

Carter looks at me appraisingly before nodding. "Thanks," he says, scratching the back of his hair. "I know I reacted strongly, and it's not like you can't have opinions. He's your son too. I just want you to think about what you say before it comes out of your mouth. Especially in front of Maya. She already questions every decision she makes about him, so just tread lightly. Please."

"I will." With that, Carter slaps my shoulder

before heading back over to JJ. I take a few moments to gather myself, rubbing at my chest to try and ease the ache I feel as I think over what Carter just told me. Maya thinking she's inadequate while burning the candle at both ends just to keep our little boy happy and healthy is hard to take. Her not being able to see how amazing she is blows me away, and I make a promise to myself to show her that truth as often as I can.

Maya emerges from the room not long after I've rejoined JJ. Her arms stretch over her head as she yawns and joins us at the table. "Hey." She ruffles JJ's hair and takes the open seat next to him. Looking over his head at me, she smiles sleepily at me. "Thanks for letting me sleep. I guess I needed it."

"I'll bet," I tell her, returning her smile. "It was nice to get to spend some time with him one on one." After our little talk, Carter grabbed his laptop and retreated to the couch, leaving JJ and me to color and work on a puzzle. It was a nice olive branch after the dressing down he gave me, and I appreciate it.

"That's fantastic," she says, just as JJ shows her the picture he made her. "Oh, I love it. Can you describe it to me?" she asks of what is essentially a giant green blob.

"Green doggy," JJ says happily. His face shifts from joy to frustration before slapping his hands on the table. "I hungee."

Maya meets my eyes and she rolls her eyes lightly. "You're always hungry," she says, kissing the top of his head before standing. "How about I set you up with a few samples before we make dinner?"

JJ nods and adds more green scribbles to his picture blob. Remembering what Carter said, I hop up and rush into the kitchen, placing my hand on the small of Maya's back while she roots around in the refrigerator.

"Why don't I help? It will be good for me to learn how to put things together for him."

Maya looks over her shoulder at me, a bright smile on her face. "I'd like that." She continued to smile at me for a moment before she starts pulling out various fruits and vegetables and placing them on the counter.

My eyes flick over to the couch and I see Carter tip his head at me, a small smile on his face. Well, it seems I've done one thing right, but it's only a start. I really need to step up my game, not only to make up for lost time, but to prove to Maya and JJ that I can be there for them. It's what I want more than anything in the world, and the desire to make it happen burns almost as brightly as my desire to be with Maya as more than a co-parent. We've been apart for too long, and I'll be damned if I let that happen again.

Chapter Fifteen
Maya

Hodgepodge is the last place I want to be today, but the world doesn't stop turning just because my baby daddy strolled back into town and threw my world into chaos. Despite all the crazy adjustments of the last two days, our time with Jake has been damn special and I would never trade it for the normality of life before. The car drive after lunch was way more affectig than I thought it would be, but it felt good to let out those emotions, the pent-up sadness over him not being here, as well as over the house that looks nothing like the one I grew up in.

Luckily, I couldn't dwell in my sadness very long. As soon as we got back to the apartment, I got to watch Jake and JJ bond more, letting their combined laughter heal some of the damage done to my heart over the last few years. The fact that Jake let me rest while they played was a nice treat too. Opportunities to catch up on rest are few and far between, so I appreciated that he felt confident enough with our son to let me, and that I felt confident enough in his ability to watch JJ and keep him safe to fall asleep in the first place.

Jake helping cut up veggies for dinner, and then him holding JJ in the kitchen while I made spaghetti was also incredible. It was like getting a window into the world we'd been denied for so long, but one we could have if we tried. Keeping myself from asking Jake about his future plans or implying that he should stay has been difficult, but I've managed to do it for the most part. Last night while we were reading JJ to sleep, I mentioned how nice it was to have him there with the two of us, and the hopeful expression on Jake's face had me wondering if I should just come right out and ask him to stay, but that seemed crazy.

We spent one day together three years ago. Societal norms dictate that I shouldn't feel as strongly about him as I do, but trying to fight my feelings is like trying to swim upstream. I'm not strong enough to keep it up nor do I really have the desire to do so. If JJ hadn't interrupted us, I'm pretty sure he would have kissed me in the car, and I could tell he wanted to kiss me last night when he left to go back to his cabin, but something is holding him back. Fear is what's holding me back. Fear of rejection is a small factor, but more than that is fear that I'll fall even more in love with him than I already am only for him to leave again. Shaking my head, I put all that out of my mind and try to focus on the present, and presently I need to open the store and start the day.

Carter has been in the workshop since early this morning, already hard at work trying to finish a couple of pieces that were ordered online, which means it will be just me manning the store until he comes to relieve me so I can put JJ down for a nap. Sue offered to watch him since she is in town, but after telling her about Jake showing up and making her promise not to interfere until I invite her over sometime, she made plans with friends instead, letting me know she would be here if I needed. I'm glad of her offer, and I may take her up on it someday so that Jake and I can be alone, but giving him time to bond with his son is more important than my need to reconnect with him on a more personal level. At least, it is for the moment.

With my son on my hip, I walk over to what used to be the office and is now essentially JJ's playroom with a small desk and a laptop in the corner. We head inside and I flick on the light, set him down at his play table with a set of giant connector blocks, and fire up the laptop to check the website for orders and emails from artisans. After scrolling through some pretty mundane stuff, my eyes brighten when I see there are five more orders for my crocheted baby booties. As excited as I am about the popularity of the items I create, I also try not to sigh at knowing that it means a few long nights so I can fulfill the orders in a timely manner. Customer reviews are the lifeblood of small businesses, and if we can't get things out on time, we don't get the five-star ratings that keep our doors open. An alarm on my phone beeps and I realize it's time to open the store. Mondays are normally a little on the slower side, especially after a big festival weekend, so maybe I can start working on one of those new orders while I play with JJ.

"Be right back, sweetheart," I tell my son, patting his head as I pass.

"Okay, Mommy." He doesn't even look up as I leave, too focused on trying to fit two blocks together, little frustrated grunts escaping his mouth as he does.

Work would be a lot easier if I didn't also have JJ with me, but daycare is more money than I care to part with. There is also the fact that I would miss him like crazy. He's been with me constantly since his birth, so I'm more than a little used to always having him around and I love every minute of it. I'm already nervous about how I'll handle him going to preschool next year. JJ will be fine, of course, so I'm not worried about him. Anytime there are other little kids around, he joins them like they've all been best friends since the womb. Me? I already know I'm going to blubber like a baby and feel at loose ends when I'm not watching over him twenty-four-seven. Until then, I'll try to enjoy the time I can.

When I get to the door, I'm surprised to see Jake standing there, a coffee holder in one hand and a white paper bag in the other. He smiles at me and nods in greeting, and after flipping the store sign to OPEN and unlocking the door, I usher him inside and out of the cold. Fall in the mountains starts cold and stays cold until about April, so I hope he packed enough sweaters and jackets for his stay. As he walks past, I catch a hint of evergreen smell, not sure if it's wafting in from outside or his cologne. If it's him, it's new, and I am enjoying it even more than I did his springtime soap smell from years earlier. No matter what scent he wears, he always smells like home and I want more of it. While he walks to the counter, I take a minute to admire the man in front of me. He's still as good-looking and athletic as before, but his pants either fit nicer or he's been focusing a lot more on his glutes because, damn if Jake doesn't have the best-looking butt I have ever seen. He turns and looks at me over his shoulder, a smirk spreading across his face. Busted.

Warmth floods through me as my cheeks heat with a blush, and I move quickly to the other side of the counter that holds the register. "I thought you were busy this morning," I mention after clearing my throat. It does nothing to clear away my desire, but I manage to push it down enough to try and behave like a responsible adult. "We weren't expecting to see much of you until after nap time." After tucking JJ in last night, we made plans to see each other today, but he mentioned needing to make a few business calls and therefore probably wouldn't be available until this afternoon.

Jake is still smirking slightly as he slides the coffee container over to me. "I was busy, but my calls went a little smoother than expected." He holds up a messenger bag that's slung over his shoulder. "I might need to do a little research and send some emails, but I figured I could do that from here and get to spend some time with the two of you while I do."

A smile spreads across my face at the thought of even more time together with this man. "That sounds terrific," I blather. I grab the paper cup with my name on the side to try and stifle some of my giddiness. Lifting the cup to my nose, I inhale the smell of bold, roasted coffee and vanilla bean, and my smile widens as I look over at Jake. "How did you know my coffee order?"

"I may have asked Carter the other day while you were changing JJ's diaper," he confesses, the tips of his ears turning pink. The shy look on his face is surprisingly sexy, almost as sexy as the fact that he's asking about my favorites to please me. The care he has shown over the last two days has my deep feelings for him taking root, becoming more and more permanent with each passing interaction.

My cheeks hurt from smiling so hard at him, but I don't want his effort to be in vain, so I break away from his gaze and sip the drink, enjoying the taste and feel of the hot liquid as it slides down my throat. "Well, thank you for thinking of me," I tell him. My hands bring the cup to my mouth once again to hide the smile that won't leave my face.

Jake shrugs a shoulder. "I'm always thinking of you, Beautiful." He says it so casually, like him thinking about me is something commonplace, something that happens all the time. That warm, fuzzy sensation that seems to be present whenever I think about or am around Jake spreads from my chest to the rest of my body, even warming the tips of my toes better than any wool socks ever could.

"That's really sweet of you to say," I manage to get out. My mind is whirring from all the thoughts and feelings flooding in at once that I'm not sure I won't burst out an "I love you" at any moment. "I-I think about you all the time too. Just so you know," I admit. My shoulder shrugs in the same manner his did as I try to play it cool when my feelings for him are anything but casual.

Jake reaches over and grabs my hand, running his thumb over my palm and sending sparks of desire through me. God, even something as little as hand-holding has my engine revving, though I know it isn't the physical contact so much as the strangely intimate connection we share despite spending such a short amount of time together. "Maya," he says, his voice low and his gaze intent. "We should talk about the future."

My mouth opens to agree with him, but JJ interrupts us with an ill-timed appearance at my side. Reminding myself how much I love my son, I turn to look down at him and see a distressed expression on his face. "What is it, baby?"

"Mommy, pee-pee," he says, squirming in his wet diaper.

"Ah, of course." Dropping my coffee on the counter, I reach down and pick him up. One thing that will be nice about preschool is that they require potty training, so at least we won't be dealing in dirty diapers come this time next year. "Let's get you cleaned up, little man." My eyes look over at Jake to see him watching us, a small smile on his face. "Want to help?" I offer. Like I said, kids aren't all sweet kisses and playtime. They're tantrums and poopy diapers and nighttime wake-ups. Jake needs to see it all, the good and the bad.

Jake's smile drops slightly, but he recovers nicely and walks over to us. "I'd love to," he says. The seemingly false cheer elicits a snort from me.

"Love might be a strong word for how much fun dirty diapers are," I tell him. We walk into the office and I set up the changing pad on the floor. "But I appreciate your enthusiasm." He's here and he's trying. That is more than enough.

Jake chuckles, shaking his head and kneeling next to me. "Maybe I don't love the diaper part so much as I like being here with you, helping you out." He finger-combs JJ's curly hair before I lay him down on the mat. "Spending time with my so—with JJ, means a lot to me," he says. The sad smile on his face after stumbling over the word "son" has me feeling all kinds of guilty. JJ is his son, and Jake should get to claim him as such. I just need to be a little more certain about things before we go there. The fact that they are father and son won't change, but I don't want to start throwing around the "Dada" label if he's just going to leave.

Needing to comfort him in some small way, I reach over and place my hand on Jake's thigh, and give it a squeeze. I ignore the fact that it's all muscle, focusing instead on providing solace and not getting a little groping in myself. "We really should talk about the future."

He nods and I start changing JJ's diaper, walking Jake through how to do it while avoiding getting a small spray from a second round, and giving him the honors of walking it to the dumpster in the back of the shop. When he comes back into the office, he has the white paper bag from earlier and he holds it up, a bashful expression on his face as he scratches along his jaw. "I, uh, got a pumpkin muffin for JJ at the coffee shop, but I wasn't sure if that would be okay with you," he says, his expression moving from bashful to earnest. "It's one of their vegan ones. I wasn't sure if he had any allergies and I didn't want to risk it. Oh, and I also brought a plastic knife to cut it up so it won't be a choking hazard."

Jake's thoughtfulness and attention to big things like allergies and choking hazards has me smiling at him. I open the tiny desk drawer and pull out a small paper plate, passing it to him and nodding at the table where JJ is sitting with his blocks. "He loves pumpkin muffins. Luckily, no allergies to speak of yet, but too much dairy does tend to upset his stomach and gives him horrible gas. Like, flee the room because it smells like death gas." I shake my head. Why does it seem that I'm either always talking about gas or poo with everyone nowadays? I need to get out more. "Sorry. That's probably too much information."

Jake's head shakes vehemently from side to side. "There's no such thing as too much information when it comes to him," he's quick to reply. As he starts setting JJ up with his tiny muffin slices, he looks over at me and smiles thoughtfully. "I want to know absolutely everything."

His words are the perfect reminder of the journals and pictures I've been keeping since pregnancy. Standing from the desk and giving a look around the empty store, I decide that now is as good a time as any to go and get them. It's important to me that Jake gets even that small window into JJ's past, so I turn to him and hold up a finger. "Are you good with him for a minute? I need to grab something from upstairs."

Jake's eyes brighten, no doubt pleased with my trust in him watching our little boy solo. "Absolutely," he says, placing another muffin piece over to JJ's plate. "We're good. Right bud?"

JJ simply stuffs a slice of muffin in his mouth while he plays with his blocks, which is as good a vote of confidence as any you'll get from him. "Thanks," I say to Jake, giving a small wave to our son. "Mommy will be back in a minute." JJ pays me no mind, clearly more invested in the delicious muffin in front of him than anything else. After shooting a small smile at Jake, I rush out the back and up the wooden staircase to the apartment, walking quickly to my bedroom and reach under the bed, grabbing the box containing the two leather-bound journals and picture book I kept for Jake. After another quick journey back downstairs, I slow my approach as I reach the office, smiling when I hear laughter coming from the small room.

"Again, again," JJ shouts. My head pops around the corner just in time to see Jake put his hand partway over his mouth and blow, creating a loud noise that sounds suspiciously close to a fart. The rumbling sound echoes around the room and JJ claps, giggling his head off. "Again, again."

Jake laughs along with him, but holds a finger up to his mouth. "Just one more, okay. I'm not sure your mommy would be happy with me making all the fart noises."

I smile and walk into the room. "As long as they're coming from the top end and not the bottom, it's fine with me," I joke. A laugh bursts from my chest at the sight of Jake looking like he just got caught with his hand in the cookie jar.

"Sorry," he sputters, but not before making one last tiny farting noise for JJ. "I figured if fake injuries worked on him, pretend flatulence might too."

With a shrug of my shoulder, I smile at him and sit across from him on the rug. "Looks like you were correct," I say, placing the box on my lap. My fingers drum across the top nervously as I try to think of the words to accompany the gift. I want Jake to have these memories, but at the same time, it's a little difficult to part with them. My fingers slide to the sides of the box and grip tightly. These memories are stored in my mind and will be for a very long time, and copies of the pictures exist on our computer, but as I finally pass the box to Jake, I feel a strange sense of loss. The past is difficult to let go of, even knowing that the only way is forward. Instead of thinking about what I'm losing, I try to think about what will be gained from this and focus on that, on the possibilities of a big, bright future for the three of us. I nod for Jake to open the box. "I know it will never be possible for you to know everything, every moment I've had with him since the beginning, but I did my best."

Jake looks puzzled as he removes the lid from the box. The confusion doesn't leave his face until he opens the cover and starts reading the first page of the first journal. "I found out I'm pregnant today, and I'm so excited. I just wish Jake was here to share it with me," he reads aloud, looking over at me with shiny eyes. "I miss him, but I know he'll come back, so this is my way of keeping him close in the meantime." He swallows thickly and looks over at me from his place on the floor. "You knew I'd come back?"

I shrug a shoulder, not wanting to get too deeply into the feels with JJ in the room. "I had a feeling," I say, blinking away tears. "I also had a pretty sure bet that if I tossed enough money into that fountain, it might happen." My joke lightens the mood, but only just.

The corner of Jake's mouth twitches and he sets the journal aside, picking up the photobook and opening it. "Wow." The words are whispered reverently as the tips of his fingers brush over the plastic sheets. He gazes at the first couple of pages which are mostly comprised of pictures of me at milestone months in the pregnancy. "You look radiant," he gushes. He turns to look up at me with an expression I would describe as awestruck, but it seems vain to think that, so I'll just assume he's filled with gratitude for my keeping the albums for him. Thinking otherwise could get my hopes up.

"Thank you," I accept graciously. My fingers

reach over to flip the page, taking the focus away from me and onto our son. The first picture is one of JJ as the reddest, grumpiest-looking newborn baby in the world. "He looks like an angry beetroot, but once they cleaned him off, he cheered up some."

"He's beautiful," Jake tells me. "Just like his mother."

I blush, but bat away the compliment with a wave of my hand. "Please. He is your mini-me and you know it." I certainly do. Every day I looked at my boy and watched him grow more and more into a carbon copy of his dad. It was wonderful and painful at the same time, but now that Jake is back, the pain has lessened considerably.

Jake shrugs and flips the page. "Maybe, but that doesn't change the fact that he's a cute kid and that you, Maya, are the most beautiful woman I have ever seen."

My breath hitches at his admission. I like to think of myself as a decent-looking person, and when he told me the same thing three years ago, I might have believed it could have been true. Years of grief, lack of sleep, and single mothering, however, has left me looking and feeling tired, washed out. It's hard not to be a little self-conscious when your body doesn't look like it used to and you feel like a different person in many ways. "I appreciate that you think that," I tell him. My body shifts uncomfortably on the rug and my eyes glance away from him so he can't see how little I think of myself these days.

Jake tucks a finger under my chin and brings my gaze back to his. "I just don't think it, Maya. I know it." He brushes his finger across my cheek. "And I'll tell you every day for the rest of my life so you know it too."

My heart picks up speed at the mention of every day forever, and speeds up even more as I watch JJ come over and climb onto Jake's lap. "Pictures," he says, pointing at the photos in the book in front of him.

Jake looks like he's holding his breath, not wanting to disturb the moment. Finally, he exhales, the brightest smile I've seen spreading across his face as he points at a photo of JJ in his crib. "That's right, bud. This is baby JJ."

"That me," JJ exclaims. His body leans down to get a closer look at the image, so much that his button nose almost touches the page. Jake adjusts the way he's sitting, cuddling JJ closer as the two of them look at the book.

Seeing another opportunity to give them some much-needed time together, I stand to go out into the store. "I'm going to let you two enjoy the photos," I say, walking over to the doorway. "I should probably do my job a little, after all." With that, I grab a feather duster and start making my way around the store.

Doing my job was also a convenient excuse to come out and gather my thoughts, settle the feelings swirling around inside me like a February blizzard. Thankfully a few customers start pouring in and give me ample time to distract myself for a bit. *The rest of my life,* is what Jake had said. I want to believe that he means it, but it's not even been two days. Hope blossoms in my chest like a rose in springtime, and I don't bother to tamp it down. Now that I've seen what life could be like with him in it, I don't want to go back to what it was before. I have no idea how to go about keeping him here, but I'll try. He already has one reason to stay—JJ. Maybe I can work a little harder to give him one more.

Chapter Sixteen
Jake

The last few days have been amazing, astounding really. My mornings are spent making calls, trying to line things up so I can move to Starlight Lake, not just to be closer to Maya and JJ, but to be with them as we were always meant to. We still haven't had our talk about the future, but I'm hoping Maya and I will get a chance to do that tomorrow night after dinner. It has snowed the last couple of days, so we've been spending most of our time inside, laughing and playing with our little boy. Maya sometimes works on the baby booties and blankets she's been using as a side hustle to make money while I build towers, color, or read with JJ. Hopefully, Maya will be able to focus on that as her full-time job like she wants to, once I'm here permanently.

I'm hoping the future we talk about includes the three of us living together as a family once I move here. Eventually, I plan to ask Maya to marry me, but I'm going to keep that to myself for now. The pull I feel toward her is magnetic, and it's even stronger now after having spent the last couple of nights reading through the journals she kept. The entries from the last year or so are mostly just bits of cute or interesting things JJ has done, a small window into the world I missed while I was in Denver. The journals of the time before that were more than a window. It was like Maya threw open the door to her thoughts and feelings, inviting me to come in and walk around in her shoes, taking in the highs and lows from her time being pregnant and from JJ's first year of life. It would have been easy to wallow in the fact that I missed so much, but reading these journals gave me a sense that I was there, experiencing every moment with her. I felt her joy at the sight of our little boy on the ultrasound screen, and I also empathized with the bone-deep tiredness she felt that fist month with a newborn. I'm not sure I've ever been that tired, but her words had me feeling the exhaustion right along with her. At least next time, she won't have to go it alone.

Kids are something I've always wanted, and we have JJ, but I think one or two more sounds like a good idea. It will have to wait a while, though. Getting to know my son better and his getting to know me is important, as is spending as much time with his mom as possible. There have been so many times over the last few days when I wanted nothing more than to pull her into my arms and kiss her until we were both senseless, but I haven't been able to act on it just yet. It seems that anytime we get close, JJ finds a way to interrupt us. It almost seems like it's on purpose, but I feel like he's taken a liking to me over the last week, so I'm sure it's just a matter of kids always being around. We get along well, and he even comes up to hug me when I visit.

The fact that he's been referring to me as "J" and not "Daddy," still chafes a bit, but I plan to bring it up later when Maya and I talk. Hopefully, what JJ calls me will get rectified soon enough. What I need to straighten out immediately is my job. I have an idea for what my career could look like from now on, but I'm not so sure my dad will go for it. The calls I've made all week have been to current clients to gauge their willingness to work with a remote consultant, and to local businesses to see how willing they would be to work with a marketing consultant to increase their customer traffic and revenue. After favorable reactions from both, I feel like I can move onto the next step.

Currently, that next step involves me sitting in the rental cabin. I told Maya I needed to make some more calls this morning, and I wasn't lying. As I gaze around at the stone- and wood-paneled walls, taking in the green sofa in the small seating area of the tiny one-bedroom as well as the deer head mounted on the wall, I try to think of the best way to approach the request I'm going to put forth to my dad. When I have a plan and put off the call as long as I can, I finally dial his number, hoping things go smoothly.

"Jake," my dad's voice booms from the other end of the phone. Alexander Mackenzie is a big man with an even bigger presence, so much so it pours through the phone, causing my nerves to stir. "How's the vacation?" He says "vacation" so distastefully it's almost funny. The man needs to relax. Maybe some time off work is something I can convince him and Mom to do once they learn about JJ. A trip to the mountains could be just the ticket to get my dad to loosen up. I would attribute my own sense of renewed energy to the fresh mountain air, but I know it's from being around Maya and my son.

"It's good. Great, actually," I tell him truthfully. "It's the reason I called." My father makes a low humming sound in the phone, already disgruntled before I've mentioned one word of my idea. He gives me the space to continue, so I do. "I have some thoughts regarding the business that I wanted to run past you."

A sound of relief pushes through the speaker. "Oh, so you're coming back early. You can call Heather to make an appointment or we can talk at dinner when you get back into town."

I chuckle humorlessly, trying to refocus the conversation. "Um, no. I'm not ending my vacation," I confess. "If anything, I'm extending it in a way. I'm hoping to open a small branch of the consulting business here in Starlight Lake."

My dad sputters for a moment, no doubt choking

on his second cup of coffee despite the fact it's only eight o'clock in the morning. "What? Starlight Lake? Where even is that?" I hear the clacking of keys over the phone and assume he's looking up my current location. "That town is the size of a postage stamp, Jacob. There is no way we're expanding to a tiny mountain town when there won't even be enough business to keep us afloat."

Summoning all my calming skills, I take a deep breath and exhale slowly. I really need this to work out, but me getting too emotional about it will be a surefire way to get him to reject my idea. "Here me out. Please, Dad." I don't ask for much, so he can give me this at least.

After a moment of taut silence, he finally speaks. "Fine." He sighs, and I get directly to the point of my plan.

"The town has a number of businesses in need of major updating, and there are a few small towns located within a short driving distance from here, so there are more opportunities literally just around the corner," I explain, keeping the conversation moving so he doesn't have a chance to interrupt. "I can still work on my same accounts remotely, and I can even drive into Denver periodically to meet with them in person on anything we can't get done electronically or via video chat."

My mind speeds along as I continue explaining some of the logistics of my idea, how I can work from home until I find a suitable office space to meet with clients, and how even though the businesses would be smaller and bring in less money, the amount of time needed to maintain their portfolio would be much less. Hell, I even offered to take a pay cut to make this happen. Thanks to my dad's advice over the years, I've made several wise investments and the three of us can live off the interest for a time should we hit a rough patch.

"Well," my dad says hesitantly. "It's an interesting plan, and while I'll need to see a more formal proposal, some hard numbers and projections, I think it could be possible. Tell me, though, Jacob, why this town? I haven't even heard of it before today."

The air whooshes out of my lungs. It's not that I'm not excited to tell my parents about JJ. I am, it's just that I hadn't planned on doing it over the phone. It's not exactly the kind of truth bomb you drop in casual conversation, not that this has resembled that even remotely. "I'd really rather do this in person, or at the very least, with Mom on the phone too."

"I'll conference her in," my father days decisively. Any hopes I had of putting off what will be a surprising but hopefully happy conversation are completely upended as I hear him dial her in.

"What is it, Alex?" my mom's voice chimes in. "I'm supposed to be meeting Kathleen for some early Christmas shopping soon."

"Hi, Mom," I say, bursting in before I can chicken out and end the call. This is too important to screw up with something as silly as a few nerves. With one last silent prayer that this conversation goes well, I continue, "I've just been talking to Dad and we thought it would be a good idea to get you on the line."

"Yes," my father says gruffly. "It seems Jacob wants to open a satellite office in some small mountain town out West." Out West makes it sound like I'll be living in the wild and not a mere three hours from where they live, and I roll my eyes at my father's dramatics.

My mother makes a choked sound. "What? I thought you were working toward a promotion. Moving wasn't part of your plan." There are those plans again. The plans of the past continue to haunt me, but instead of sticking to what I thought was best for me more than a decade ago, I'm going to do what's best for me and my small family now.

"I came up with that plan when I was seventeen, Mom. Plans change. People change," I tell her, admitting that I have changed. Being with Maya changed me, and while I tried for three years to stubbornly stick to being the person I used to be, I should have been embracing the person I want to be, the person I felt like when I was with her. The kind of person that breaks plans to experience new things, the kind of person that believes in magic. If not the supernatural kind, then the kind that comes from meeting that one special person that makes you feel seen in ways no one else has. That's the kind of magic I felt with Maya, and I want to experience it every chance I get. After taking a deep breath, I proceed to download a much-shortened version of the story to them. How I met Maya, fell in love with her instantly, left and tried to go back to life as usual, and how when I came back to her three years later, I discovered I had a child. They have a grandson.

"What's his name? What does he look like?" my mother asks. There is a bit of excitement in her voice even though I know she's probably a little disappointed that I'm not following the path they helped guide me to take. Grandkids go a long way toward smoothing things over it seems.

Thinking about my beautiful little boy has me grinning. "His name is JJ, short for Jacob Johansen, and he looks pretty much like any picture you have of me as a two-year-old. He's all red curls, big smiles, and an even bigger heart." I swallow thickly, at danger of being overcome by just how happy I am. "You're going to love him as much as I do."

I hear my mom sniffle. "He sounds lovely. I'm sure we will."

"Of course we will. He's our grandson," my father says gruffly. A loaded silence hangs over the phone as I wait for my dad to give me the green light on my idea. "I can tell this means a lot to you, and in no way do I want to keep you from your son, but as much as I want to just say yes to what you're asking, Jacob, I can't make a business decision based on emotion or nepotism. You may have changed, but I certainly haven't. I don't feel right saying yes to this without going through proper procedure."

I nod even though I am alone in the room and exhale the breath I'd been holding while I waited for his decision. "Okay. I'll put together a formal business plan and come back into the city to present it to you and Anton. I'll schedule with Heather as soon as I have a date worked out." I'm already mentally starting to put things together, but there's one last thing I need to mention before I get off the phone. "Oh, and Dad, thanks for the opportunity."

My father scoffs, offended at my thinking he wouldn't hear me out, even though we both know that has happened in the past. "You don't need to thank me. Just work on that plan because as much as I feel like I'm going to end up losing money on it, I really want to say yes." He pauses for a moment, a heavy breath coming through the line. "I want you to be able to take care of our grandbaby."

"So do I," I tell them. After promising to send lots of pictures and give plenty of details about JJ to them over the coming days, I hang up the phone. About two minutes later, my mother texts, telling me to ask Maya when they can come for a visit. I laugh at that because as much as my parents were all about schedules and routines for me, I have the feeling they are going to be a lot looser when it comes to my kid. Spontaneous trips to the mountains to come see him, late bedtimes, unlimited sugar, and buying him whatever he wants are just a few of the things I can already imagine them doing.

With that call out of the way, I decide that taking the next few hours to work on my business plan is probably the best use of my time. I would try to work at Hodgepodge, but with both Maya and JJ there, I will get next to nothing accomplished. I shoot off a quick text, letting Maya know I'll be there for lunch and set my phone aside, wanting all my focus to be on this plan. The future I want to create with Maya depends on it.

Chapter Seventeen
Maya

Sundays are always the best, and not just because I don't have to go into the store for work. Sunday is my favorite day of the week because I get to spend the whole day with my son, and now Jake too. Jake came early this morning, bringing a box of donuts from the small place down the street and a stuffed dragon for JJ. It's green, of course, and our little guy took to it immediately, snuggling it tightly and thanking Jake with the biggest hug yet. Breaking the news to JJ that Jake is his dad is something that has been on my to-do list for the past day or so, but I haven't had a chance to talk to Jake about our future together yet. We had planned to last night, but JJ was having a difficult time sleeping and wouldn't stay in his bed unless I stayed there with him. Jake said he understood and went back to his rental, and while every part of me wanted to beg him to stay, I let him go, sticking to the routine we've become accustomed to just to keep things simple.

It's kind of funny, how our roles have reversed a bit. Now it's me talking about getting upstairs for naps and eating dinner around the same time while Jake has totally embraced the unpredictability that comes with any toddler. No matter what our son's mood, Jake just rolls with it, trying to comfort him if he's upset or make him laugh when he's happy. He also seems to be fine with the times we've almost kissed and gotten interrupted by our kid while I am going crazy with the need to just make it happen. It's roughly thirty degrees outside every day, but I might as well be walking around in a bikini for all the cold I feel. My skin is hot and itchy, my palms sweat with nerves, and my hands twitch with the need to explore his body. More than all that, though, there is such an ache in my lower belly from how my body craves to be with him that the number of times I've had to excuse myself to the bathroom to splash cold water on my face would be hilarious if it weren't so damned frustrating.

Even now as Jake slices veggies up for JJ to snack on while Carter makes dinner, I'm leaning against the counter, drooling at the sight of the sturdy forearms poking out from beneath the sleeves of his sweater. When he bends over to pick up a carrot that rolled off the ledge, I bite down on my lower lip to keep from whimpering at the sight of that tight rear end, perfectly encased in a pair of dark-wash jeans that look good on him but would look even better on the floor of my bedroom. Damn it. The man has me so twisted up I'm even thinking cheesy pick-up lines in my head.

"Mommy uppy?" JJ asks from beside me. Grateful for the thought interruption, I smile and pick him up while willing myself to calm down. JJ is a nice reminder to keep it in my pants, metaphorically and physically. Until we have the future squared away, there's no use in me lusting after a man who may never be mine.

Carter pops into view as he drains the pasta over the sink, ending my lustful thoughts once and for all. My brother has been supportive of the time I'm spending with Jake, but he's warned me not to get caught up in the magic like I did last time, at least not until I know what the plan is. "Dinner should be ready in a few. Sue texted me about ten minutes ago saying she would be a little late and to not wait on her to start eating."

I snort. "Yeah, okay, Sue," I say sarcastically. Bouncing JJ on my hip as Jake offers him a toddler-sized bite of carrot, I roll my eyes at my honorary aunt's words. Sue may be the one of the most helpful people on the planet, and she has helped Carter and I through our grief as best she could while not living in the same town, but she is a stickler for certain things.

"Why do you sound like she'll be mad if we eat before she gets here?" Jake asks, popping a small bit of carrot into his mouth. As I am momentarily distracted by the sight of Jake's full lips moving together like I want them to be doing all over me, Carter chimes in for me.

"Even though she is the one running late, Sue would consider it the height of impropriety if we were to dine without her," Carter says in a haughty accent. "Probably something she picked up from all those Regency romance novels she reads." Carter dumps the drained pasta into the sauce and gives it a stir.

"I read those too and you won't see me holding anyone up from their meal, especially not a two-year-old." I tweak JJ's nose, earning a small giggle from my baby. "It's a good thing Daddy is cutting up some samples for you, huh?" I say. The realization of what just came out of my mouth hits only when I see both Carter and Jake staring at me. My breath quickens and my heart races. I hadn't planned on just blurting it out like that, but maybe this will be a good thing.

"Here you go, bud. I got a little cucumber for you," Jake says, saving me from my panic spiral. When our eyes meet, he nods and smiles, telling me with one look that the slip-up was okay and he won't hold me to what I said. My heartbeat slows, but my mind doesn't. Don't I want him to hold me to it? JJ needs his daddy, and that's what Jake is. It's what our son should call him.

Twenty minutes later, Sue has arrived and the five of us sit at the table to enjoy our meal, the "Daddy" incident forgotten for the time being. "So, Jake," Sue starts. From her expression, it seems she's ready to begin another round of asking Jake as many questions as she possibly can. "You're a business consultant, right? What would you recommend I do to drum up more business for my medical equipment company?"

Jake wipes his mouth with a cloth napkin and takes a sip of water before answering her. After narrowing his gaze slightly, his eyes flicker to me for a moment before they move back to her. "Well, not knowing your business very much, I would assume it's absolutely perfect and doesn't need one single change," he tells her with a smile.

Sue barks and laugh and slaps her hand on the table. "Okay. Now tell me how you really feel because as much as I would like to, I'm not falling for that baloney." Sue has always been a sassy lady, and I know her heart is in the right place, but it feels like she's testing Jake when I'm trying to make things easier so he'll stay.

"Very well," Jake tells her, leaning forward in his chair slightly. "As I mentioned, I don't know anything about your business specifically, but if you really want to make more sales you could look at the social media accounts. As much as it might pain some people to hear it, that kind of marketing is a necessary part of doing business these days, even with something as crucial as medical equipment."

"You mean I have to start filming myself dancing around like some crazy person on plip-plop, or clock stop, or whatever you kids call it?" Hearing Sue refer to two thirty-year-olds and a twenty-six-year-old as kids is funny. I use social media for the store, but even I'm not brave enough to do any of those viral dance crazes just to get more traffic.

Jake shakes his head and grabs a slice of garlic bread from the basket on the table. "I don't think you need to go that far, though I'm sure these three would get a kick out of it," he says, waving the bread around the table. "What I mean is, posting pictures or videos of your supplies in use. Maybe get some testimonials about just how helpful it can be. Let people get to know what goes on after the sale. Why not use that to your advantage and sell them a story that will warm their hearts at the same time it opens their wallets?"

Sue nods thoughtfully before grabbing some garlic bread for herself. "Not a bad idea, Mister." She bites into the slice and chews heavily. "If I do that and see enough increase in business, I'll even name our bestselling bedpan after you."

Jake chuckles and holds up a hand. "Thank you, but there's no need for that. I enjoy helping people grow their business. It's part of why I went into consulting." He looks over at me and smiles sweetly. "Besides. You're important to Maya, so you doing well is important to me."

I blush under his and everyone else's attention. Grabbing JJ's plate, I make a beeline for the kitchen and busy myself with restocking his supply of cut veggies even though I'm sure he's done for the night.

My body stiffens as I feel a presence at my back. "I didn't mean to make you uncomfortable," Jake whispers from behind me. His hand rests on the small of my back like it has been over the last week. It's a comforting gesture and I feel myself sinking into it. It's also a possessive one and I am enjoying feeling like I belong to him more than I should, especially since we haven't talked yet.

My body turns to face him like it always does, finding its true north and wanting to stay pointed there always. "You didn't," I admit, biting my lower lip for a moment. "We need to talk. Will you stay? Even if JJ takes forever to go to sleep, even if I have to lay in there for an hour with him, will you stay so we can figure things out?"

Jake nods and rubs his hands up and down my arms. "Of course I'll stay." I wish it was the answer to the question I'm afraid to ask, but that will have to wait at least until we get our little boy settled for the night.

We rejoin the table and finish our meal. Jake manages to keep up with Sue's continued question-and-answer session as well as Carter weirdly asking about how his friend Billie is doing until finally JJ yawns and I happily call and end to the evening. After saying goodbye to Sue and helping Carter with the dishes, we get JJ ready for bed and settle in with a story. "...and they lived happily ever after," Jake says, closing the fairy tale book and sliding it back onto JJ's shelf. I lean over and kiss our little guy on the cheek, smoothing a hand over his head. "Love you, little man."

"Love oo, Mommy," he replies, yawning widely as his eyes grow heavy.

I switch spots with Jake, taking a mental picture of the two of them together as Jake leans over and kisses JJ's forehead. "Love you, bud," he tells our son.

"Love oo too," JJ says before rolling over. Jake is stock still, watching over our little boy as he falls asleep. Finally, when he looks over to me, I see his eyes shining with moisture, and he has the most beautiful smile on his face.

After we stand and sneak out of the room, we move to the sofa. My eyes roam over to see Carter's bedroom door is closed, and I'm thankful to him for giving us the privacy. "That was incredible," Jake says quietly, a dreamy expression on his face. His eyes meet mine and he shrugs. "He probably says that to everyone, huh?"

I want to erase the now downtrodden look on his face so badly, and luckily I won't have to lie to him to do it. "No, Jake. He says it to me and Carter, and very rarely he'll even say it to Sue, but that's it," I tell him, enjoying the smile come back across his face. "He might not know what love means exactly, but to him, it means he knows you care about him enough to spend time with him, and he cares about and enjoys spending time with you too."

Jake inhales, the sound slightly shuttering as he does. "Wow," he says, clasping his hands together. "I don't think anything will ever feel as good as hearing that." He reaches over and grabs my hand, interlacing our fingers together. "Well, almost anything."

I look down at our joined hands and smile. "I know it was a bit of a slip-up earlier, but I do think we can start referring to you as Daddy," I say, licking my suddenly dry lips. "If you plan on being a part of his life, that is." My stomach drops at the idea that he might not, and I try to prepare myself to hear the worst despite Jake saying otherwise all week. I trust him and trust that he *wants* to stay, just not that he *can* stay.

Jake leans back, looking as if I just slapped him in the face. "Of course I'm going to be a part of his life, Maya." His face looks hard and he shakes his head as he looks away from me. When his eyes meet mine again, they're a deep blue and his expression has softened a bit. "I'm sorry," he says and sighs. "You asked a totally fair question. I guess it's my fault for not being much clearer before."

My shoulders fall and I try to be a little more sympathetic to what he's dealing with too. I had eight months to come to terms with the fact that my life was forever changed before JJ arrived. Jake's had to absorb all that almost instantly. "No, I'm sorry," I confess as I reach over and touch his arm. "I know it's a lot to deal with and process. I'm just eager to know what your plans are." I scoot closer with a wry smile on my face.

Jake stares into my eyes for a moment, not saying a word, but I don't squirm under his gaze because I know he's not scrutinizing or judging me. I've caught him looking at me the same way a few times this week, like he wants to look at me just because he can, and I want so badly to believe that's the case. *"I wish I could keep you."* His words from years ago run through my mind as we look at one another. Instead of remembering his actions that morning, maybe I need to focus a little more on his words from back then, and the ones he's been telling me all week. "I want to be a part of JJ's life," he says adamantly, pulling our joined hands onto his lap. "I want to be a part of both of your lives. I don't want to say too much because there's a chance it won't work out and I'll have to come up with something else, but I've been working on a plan so I can stay here. Permanently."

Hope flares in my chest, the torch I've been carrying for him all these years flaming brighter. "Here, as in Starlight Lake?"

Jake nods, gripping my hands tightly. "Yes, in the town, but also with the two of you." His eyes flick away, like he's got a secret or something, but soon his eyes are back on mine. "I know it's fast, but I want the three of us to be a family."

The flame inside my chest threatens to grow into an all-out inferno, but I temper my excitement. Jake is a good guy. He has "Always Does the Right Thing" practically written across his forehead. I don't want him to be with me out of some sense of obligation. "Jake, you'll always be JJ's dad and you'll always have a place with him," I say, trying to brush away the pain I feel at thinking of not being with him. "You don't need to include me because you feel like you have to. We can co-parent, or work something else out—"

Jake stops my words with a finger to my mouth

before he takes his strong hands and frames my face with them, his gaze boring into mine so intensely I get that otherworldly feeling again, like he's seeing into my soul. It's like part of him is recognizing the part of me that has been connected over the ages, even though we can't remember our past lives together. "Have to," he says. His head shakes in such a way, it's as if I just said the most offensive thing in the word. "Beautiful, being with you would be the privilege of a lifetime." I lean into his touch, letting the feel of his warm hand against my skin ground me. "Do you not know how incredible you are?"

Before I get a chance to reply, Jake's lips are on mine, soft and supple. It's like the touch of a butterfly's wings, but soon his hands move to the back of my neck and the kiss goes from sweet to hungry in no time. I grab onto his arms, enjoying the feel of his strong muscles beneath me. When he drives his tongue into my mouth, I open eagerly. Waiting for another kiss from him has been like wandering through the desert without water, but now I've reached my oasis and I don't plan on leaving anytime soon. Our tongues slip and slide together as we familiarize ourselves with each other again. It's just as incredible as I remember, yet somehow so much better. Jake's hands tangle into my hair and I slide mine up to his shoulders before I twist on the couch and straddle him. A pleased grunt is his only reply as I move my body as close to him as possible. When I feel his hardness underneath me, I grind down automatically, loving the friction but hating that it's caused him to pull back from me.

As our breathing mingles, I slide back and rest my bottom on his thighs. "Sorry," I say sheepishly, looking to the side and swallowing thickly. "Must have gotten carried away."

Jake tucks a finger under my chin and steers my

face back to his. "Don't be sorry, Beautiful. I like you getting carried away," he says with a small smirk, nodding at the closed bedroom doors. "I just don't love the idea of any surprise spectators."

"Oh." I slide to the side and rest my head against his shoulder. "JJ's timing has been pretty impeccable when it comes to interrupting us this week, hasn't it?"

"It has," Jake says, wrapping his arm around me. "What do you say to a date night? Just the two of us." He leans his head against mine and breathes in peacefully. "I like the idea of having you all to myself for a while. Do you think you can find a sitter for JJ for tomorrow night?"

I smile at the idea of a date. We've never really had one, which is kind of crazy for two people who share a child and love one another, though we haven't said that last part to each other just yet. Soon, I hope. "I think I can swing a sitter. If Sue can't, I'm sure Carter will be more than happy to do it." He has complained a little about not seeing his nephew as much this week, but he understands how important it is for Jake to have time with his son.

"Great. Then it's a date," he says. The two of us stay together on the couch for a bit, not really talking but just enjoying the feel of being next to one another in the quiet and stillness of the night. Eventually, Jake has to go back to his cabin and after another scorching kiss good night at the door, I sneak into my room, checking on JJ one last time before I slip under the covers. It doesn't take long for me to slip away peacefully into sleep, thoughts of Jake and us being a family on my mind, giving me sweet dreams that will hopefully soon come true.

Chapter Eighteen
Jake

Trying to think of the perfect date to take Maya on kept me up longer than I would have liked, but just before I fell asleep last night, the best idea came to me. Maya loves the holiday lights downtown, so first we'll have dinner at this little French place I saw on my drive over to Hodgepodge the other day, then we'll hit the downtown ice rink for some skating followed by a cup of hot chocolate while we sit and enjoy the cool night air. While I am not planning on her coming back to my rental cabin, I'm not *not* planning it either as evidenced by my cleaning up and requesting that Housekeeping come in while I'm gone today, ensuring that the place will look as good as possible in case we do end up back here. If that does happen, it would most likely be just to talk more, but I may have made a trip to the convenience store late last night, making a purchase of definitely not-expired condoms to be prepared just in case things go the way I hope they do.

Kissing Maya last night was wonderful, and when she straddled my lap, my erection went from half-mast to painfully hard in about zero-point-two seconds. It took every ounce of willpower and good sense I had to stop things right then. Scarring our kid for life would have been bad enough, but having her brother come out would have been worse. Carter has been friendly enough, but something tells me him finding us in that kind of position would put me back to square one with him. It's not his fault that he would think that way. After all, he doesn't know my plans. Plans that include a rather large purchase in a certain neighborhood we drove through earlier this week, as well as another from a jewelry store in Denver as soon as I go back to present my business plan to my father.

Having to put together the formal business plan is a priority, but taking Maya out on a date is a bigger one. We've done things a little backward so far. We met, fell instantly in love, at least on my part, and then we had a child together all before going out on a single date. The night we met and spent together all those years ago seemed like destiny more than anything else, and while a traditional date seems a little unnecessary when what I feel for her is already so deeply rooted in my heart and soul, we need to have some time just the two of us. That is later, though. Right now, I'm heading into Hodgepodge to spend another day with my girl and my little boy. Smiling, I walk into the shop just like I have every day for the past week. I have Maya's and my coffee order and a muffin for JJ. After the way he attacked the blueberry yesterday, I felt like a repeat of that flavor was in order.

After opening the front door and striding inside, I make my way over to the office, only to stop short at the sight of my best friend leaning over the counter, talking and laughing with Maya. Maya's eyes flick to me and her smile brightens, making my day that much better already. Still, I approach cautiously. With Billie, you never know what kind of story she's in the middle of, and I have walked in on one too many that included details from one of her hookups. "Hey," I say slowly, thankful they seem to be at a break in their conversation. After putting the coffee and paper bag down on the counter, I pull Billie in for a hug. "What are you doing here?" I ask. It's not that I'm unhappy to see her, it's just unexpected, and I hope she doesn't want to hang out. As much as I love my best friend, my plans with Maya will be broken for nothing but an emergency with our son.

Billie steps back with a perplexed expression.

"Um, why wouldn't I be here?" She looks at Maya and rolls her eyes. "When you texted about your big plan, I figured I would come and help you put it together."

I hold in my groan as I watch Maya's eyes widen. "Big plan?" she asks, looking at me hopefully. It's not a secret, but still. I don't want to get her hopes up if my dad doesn't go for it.

Billie winces. "Sorry. Was I not supposed to say anything?"

I wave off her concern. No reason to make her feel bad when there's nothing we can do about it now. "No, its fine," I tell her before turning to Maya. "It's what we talked about last night. I'm working on something, but it's not a sure thing."

"Not yet," Billie chimes in, a smirk on her face. "Now that I am here to add a little razzle-dazzle to your presentation, your chances of success just increased exponentially."

I bark a laugh. "Wow. You are either severely underestimating my abilities or insanely overestimating your own. Either way, I'll take the help." I won't have a ton of time today to work with her, but you can be damn certain I will use every tool at my disposal if it means the chances of me staying with Maya and JJ increase.

"Good." Billie looks around the shop, rubbing her hands together in a comic book evil villain fashion. "Now, where is my nephew? I have two years of tickling and cheek pinching to make up for."

Maya looks at her remorsefully, her eyes flicking to me as well. "I'm sorry," she tells us apologetically. "Our Aunt Sue came by earlier today and picked him up. She hasn't had much time with him this visit, and since I have a few things I need to catch up on and Carter is busy working on a big project, I figured it was as good a time as any for the two of them to hang out." She smiles sadly at me. "I'm sorry, I should have texted."

"No worries," I tell her, sliding her drink and the bag over. "The muffin is yours now." While I'll miss time with my boy, it's probably good for me to get used to sharing him with others. How could anyone not want to hang out with such an incredible kid?

Speaking of which, as I look over at Billie, I can see she's looking slightly deflated. "Okay," she says sadly. The expression on her face closely resembles one she would have when she was little and would pout to get her way. "I guess I can wait a little longer." My gaze flicks to Maya and we share a smile, but a low whistle next to me pulls my attention back to Billie who is staring wide-eyed at Carter as he walks into the back of the store. Despite the fact it's forty degrees outside, his hair is dark and his white t-shirt clings to his body from sweat. Whatever project he's working on, it must be a doozey because he looks exhausted. "Well, hello…"

Carter heads right into the office and comes back out moments later chugging water from a bottle. When he's done, he nods a greeting to me before his gaze wanders over to Billie. "Oh, it's you," he says, not unpleasantly.

Billie preens under his gaze. "That memorable, am I?" she asks. She smiles brightly and reaches her hand across the counter. "We didn't get to formally meet last week. I'm Billie, friend of Jake's and big fan of yours."

Carter shakes her hand as he narrows his eyes at her. "Big fan? Have we met before? I mean, other than last week." He tilts his head to the side. "I don't think I would forget someone like you." His eyes widening tells me the admission was a slip-up on his part, as does the deepening blush on his cheeks.

Billie twists her body, tilting her head to the side and fluttering her eyelashes in a move I recognize as flirting, and I make a mental note to warn her away from Cater. Billie isn't one for commitment and the last thing I need is for her to make things messy with Maya's brother. "No, we haven't met, but I've been following your work," she tells him, giving him an obvious once-over. "You may remember me from such social media comments as 'lose the flannel' and 'show us the goods.'"

Carter drops her hand and steps back, his already flushed cheeks becoming more so. "Oh, I see," he says, sounding slightly disappointed. "I would apologize for blocking you, but I don't really enjoy being teased." He clears his throat, looking uncomfortable as Maya rubs his back for a moment.

Billie chuckles lightly. "Oh, while I can most certainly be a tease, I meant every word I typed," she tells him. She shoots another flirty glance his way and leans closer to him. "There's a market out there for women who would love to see a little shirtless woodworking action, and I am one of them. If you need someone to take the pictures, or better yet, some video, do let me know. I have a Ring Light and a very vivid imagination."

"Billie," I warn. She doesn't bother looking at me as she waves me off with a flick of her wrist.

"I'll, uh, keep that in mind," Carter says, coughing into his fist. He cheeks are still red, but I don't think it's from the exertion of his work out in the shed.

"Please do," Billie tells him with a wink. She soon shifts back to her slightly pouty face and blinks up at him. "In the meantime, do you think you could unblock me? I really am a fan of the stuff you make."

Carter nods thoughtfully before nodding his head to the back of the store. "Do you, um, maybe want to see what I'm working on right now?"

Billie's eyes widen and the flirty act drops. She smiles genuinely over at Carter, not using one of the phony smiles she sometimes plasters on for just about everyone else in the world. "Hell, yes, I would." She shoves her purse at me to hold and the two of them walk out the back and over to Carter's workshop.

With a heavy sigh, I turn to Maya and grimace. "I'll try to reign her in a little when it comes to him." Billie is a man-eater and the last thing I need is one more complication in the form of her chewing Carter up only to spit him out. "She can be a bit much."

Maya snorts, a smile on her face. "Oh, please don't," she says with a chuckle. "Let her have all the fun she wants. If we're lucky, Carter will have a little too. Lord knows he needs it."

Wanting no more talk of my friend or her brother, I tuck a finger under her chin and lift her face toward mine. "And what do you need, Beautiful?" I ask, loving the way her expression goes soft when she looks at me. "Name it and I'll give it to you." I have a lot of time to make up for, and I plan on giving her the world.

"I just need you," she says. Bracing herself on the counter, she leans over and lightly brushes her lips against mine. With the counter between us, there's not much we can do beyond a few gentle kisses, but that's okay. I plan on saving up for later anyway. When Maya leans back, her eyes looked dazed, reflecting how I feel inside. I don't have a way with words, but her kisses have me wanting to spout poetry about love and beauty and happily ever after.

Making my way around the counter, I pull her into my arms to show her a little more of the poetry I'm feeling when Billie comes back into the store, shaking her head in frustration. Maya tries to step back, but I pull her close and tuck her into my side where she belongs. She may not feel confident enough to be as public about us as I am, but she will be soon. "Jeez, you turn on one table saw and the man kicks you out," she fumes, one hand propped on her hip. "I was just trying to see how it worked."

Maya makes a *yikes* expression and shrugs a shoulder. "Yeah. Carter has always been good about safety in the workshop, but he's gotten even more vigilant since…" she trails off. There's no need for her to say the words aloud for me to know she means since they lost her parents. "He won't let JJ anywhere near there, which I appreciate because I kind of like our little boy having all his fingers and toes."

"Me too," I say. My arm pulls her closer to kiss the top of her head and hopefully provide a little comfort for any sadness thinking about her parents might have brought up.

"Aww," Billie says, a wistful smile on her face. "You guys are cute."

I smile at the compliment and the bashful look on Maya's face. "We are." I lean down and give Maya one last kiss on the temple. "Since you have work to catch up on and Billie here showed up out of nowhere," I explain, glaring at my best friend. There's no malice in it, but a heads up from her would have been nice. "Why don't we work somewhere else today and I'll see you later for our date?"

"Really?" Maya asks, looking a little down. "I'm sure I can still concentrate while you two work on your plan." Seeing her disappointed expression has me wanting to change my mind, but even after those few kisses, she's not the one I'm really worried about staying on task.

"I appreciate the offer to stay," I tell her. Stepping back, I look her up and down before looking pointedly at her face. "But I don't think I'd be able to concentrate."

Billie makes a throaty sound next to us. "Gross,"

she says, grabbing her purse from where I dropped it on the counter. "Save it for another time, Romeo. Bye, Maya." I chuckle and smile at Maya as Billie pushes me out the door and into the chilly midmorning air.

As we walk over to Billie's sports car, I reach over and lightly punch her on the shoulder. "Thanks for coming," I tell her, opening the passenger door of the shiny red car and slipping inside.

"You're welcome," she says. She looks at me for a moment as she turns on the car. "I know you need help, even though you would never ask for it."

As she starts to drive toward the cabin, I realize that she might be expecting to stay with me, something that would put a definite stop to things going anywhere physical with Maya tonight. "So, did you want to bunk with me again, or…?"

Billie scoffs, giving me some serious side-eye. "Even if I did want to stay in your cabin, which I do *not*, that place is like a monument to taxidermy with all the heads on the walls." I watch her visibly shudder before she points out the window to a historic-looking hotel. "I'm staying there for the time being. They might not have an on-call masseuse like I was hoping for, but the room has a flat screen and not a stuffed squirrel in sight. Besides," she says with a smirk, "I saw you and Maya looking all gooey-eyed at one another. I know where things are headed and I want to be as far away as possible."

"Thank you," I tell her sincerely. Billie may be known as a selfish party girl, but the selfish part couldn't be further from the truth. She is always thinking of others, and it's a shame more people don't see that. "You're a good friend."

"Duh," she sasses, a smirk on her face. "And you're welcome." Billie increases her speed as we leave the downtown area. "Now, walk me through your business plan so I can poke holes in it and tell you how boring it sounds."

I laugh and tell her all about my business plan, as well as a few other plans I have for my future. Plans that include one special little boy, and one very special woman who I cannot wait to spend the evening with.

Chapter Nineteen
Maya

After spending most of the day helping customers, catching up on emails, and working on a few of my crochet projects, I finally made it upstairs with just enough time to get ready for my date with Jake tonight. There was really no need to ask him how to dress. It's cold out, and whether we're inside or outside, the occasion calls for warm clothes. After a quick shower, I head over to my dresser and pull out some fleece-lined black leggings and a gray sweater. When I get to my underwear drawer, I groan when I see the complete lack of anything even remotely sexy. I'm not planning on us sleeping together tonight, but if it happened I wouldn't be upset about it. What is upsetting is the fact that if we do end up getting naked, I'll be showing off a pair of pink cotton briefs with a mismatched blue bra. "Oh, well." Pushing my worries about being sexy aside for now, I get dressed.

Fully dressed and feeling slightly better about myself, I march into the bathroom and start to style my hair, or attempt to anyway. "Mommy, uppy," JJ calls to me from the doorway as I'm pulling a brush through my long hair.

"Mommy's getting ready for a date, little man," I tell him. When I look over and see the hopeful look on his face, I cave and grab him, setting him on the counter and handing over a clean makeup brush to play with. "You can watch Mommy put on her makeup. Hopefully she hasn't forgotten how to do it because it's been more than a little while." The last time I wore makeup was sometime during pregnancy. After a certain point, my body ached and I was just too tired to bother with it and never really picked up the habit again.

After getting my hair sorted as best as I can for someone in dire need of a haircut, I start in on some eye shadow, laughing when JJ tries to copy my movements with the oversized brush I gave him. "Here, baby. Keep it out of your eyes." I show him how to swipe the brush gently across his cheeks and he laughs as it tickles his sensitive skin. "There you go."

"Makeup at two years old?" Carter asks, clucking his tongue from just outside the bathroom. "Mom would be appalled."

I smile at the mention of our mom. Even though it's still not easy, talking about our parents has become a lot less painful over the years. "There's no makeup on it," I tell him. "Even though she made me wait until I was fourteen, you know she would make an exception for him."

Carter smiles sadly. "Yeah, she would be spoiling him rotten every chance she got." When he sees my misty eyes, he winces. "Sorry, Mai. I wasn't trying to make you sad."

Managing to blink the moisture away, I reach over and pat his arm. "It's fine," I tell him. After releasing a slow breath, I turn and resume my work in front of the mirror. It's hard not to think about how much my parents are missing out on or how much my son would have loved them, but focusing on the present helps. It might also help if we spoke of them more often than we do now. "I know it's hard, but I actually miss talking about them."

Carter nods. "Same. Let's try to do it more," he says, kicking at the tile with a socked foot. "I know I haven't dealt with it as well as I could have, but I want to try and do better."

"That sounds nice, and I'll try to do better too." I

say, just as there's a knock at the door. "Crap." JJ repeats my word and I close my eyes tightly. He'll probably drop it from his vocabulary soon enough, and it could have been much worse, but still. "Okay, baby. You go with Caju and I'll be back to say bye-bye in a minute." Once JJ is safely in Carter's care, I rush into my room and throw on a pair of wool socks and my boots.

When I step out of the room, Jake is inside, already holding onto JJ and pulling silly faces to make him smile. Jake playing with our son is sexy enough, but when you add on to that the tight jeans, light-brown sweater that pulls across his chest, and green coat that's fitted enough to cling to his biceps, the man is downright dangerous to my already accelerating libido. As I walk over to two of them, Jake's eyes meet mine and they darken a bit as they rake up and down my body, showing me he's just as affected by me as I am him. "Hey, Beautiful," he says, leaning over and kissing my cheek. "You ready to go?"

I nod before holding out my arms to JJ to give him the biggest hug imaginable. There have been times we've been apart, but it doesn't happen often, so leaving him is still a little difficult. "Okay, little man. Have fun with your uncle and be good like I know you always are. I love you."

"Wuv oo, Mommy," he says before I pass him over to Carter.

Jake leans over and gives him a little goodbye hug too before he grabs my coat and holds it open for me. With one more final wave to our little boy, we head out the door and descend the stairs to the parking lot behind the store. Jake opens the passenger door for me and I slip inside, running a hand over the soft leather as Jake climbs in on his side. "Nice ride," I comment, looking over at Jake to see him shrug a shoulder.

"I do all right," he says with a wink before starting the car. He does more than all right, but it's not the fancy car or clothes I'm interested in. It's the man behind all that I want. The man who is thoughtful, attentive, and so very fine that I don't think I'll be able to make it through dinner without wanting to jump him. "Do you like French food?" he asks, driving out toward the edge of town. "I had a place in mind, but we can go wherever you want. Tonight is all about you."

I smile at his words, and reach over to grab his hand, holding it tightly as my arms rest on the console separating us. Even that small touch has my skin warming up even more than it already is, but tonight is about more than sex and I need to remember that. "I do like French food, but how about we make tonight all about us? So, if you aren't a fan, we should pass."

Jake shakes his head, smiling at me as he pulls into a spot in front of Belle Nuit, the nicest restaurant in town. I would worry about being underdressed, but luckily we're still in the mountains of Colorado, so it's not like there's much of a dress code besides dress for the weather and be sure to leave your pet elk at home. "I should have known you weren't going to let me spoil you." Jake shakes his head at me with a smile as he leaves the car and comes over to open my door for me.

I place my hand in the one he offers as he helps me out of the SUV. Since we're alone and in no danger of being interrupted, I take the opportunity to lean into him and rest my hands on his chest. As much as I want to go out on this date, there's something I want more. It's not in me to normally be so bold, but I have wanted him for so long. I need a little something to hold me over until I get exactly what I want. "How about we have some food and then go back to your place and spoil each other?" I brush my lips against his in a kiss and pull back to see Jake's eyes darken and hear something that sounds suspiciously like a growl come from his chest. "Unless you have other plans," I say, smirking at the look of untethered need on his face.

"Plans change," he says gruffly, tugging on my hand and quickly pulling me through the doors of the restaurant. After removing our coats and following the hostess to a table that looks out onto the lake, we take a seat, staring across at one another, barely hiding our desire to eat and leave as quickly as possible.

Needing a distraction from the man across from me, I gaze around the restaurant and admire the pale-blue walls and gorgeous artwork but have to stop when Jake appears in front of me. He's taken his chair and pulled it to my side of the small table and wrapped his arm around my shoulder. "Needed a better view of the lake, did you?" I ask, a hint of teasing in my voice.

"I have the best view right here," he explains. He doesn't even bother to keep his voice low as he runs his hand up and down my neck in long, languid strokes, causing goose bumps to break out all over my skin. My eyes widen and dart to the couple across from us, only to see the older woman smile and nod her approval before turning back to her dining companion. Well, if they don't care, I certainly don't, so I lean into his touch only to pull back when our waiter shows up.

After ordering a dinner of ratatouille and roast chicken to share, we resume our canoodling while we wait for the food to arrive. The hand that isn't currently sending shivers up and down my spine with every swipe along my neck rests on the table, and I reach up and stroke the back of it, noticing the raised skin of a scar running through the dusting of copper hair. "What happened here?" I ask.

Jake chuckles lightly, flipping his hand over so he

can hold onto mine. "That is from one of the few times I didn't follow my parents' schedule for me," he says with a smile. "I was twelve, and I was supposed to be in karate, or maybe it was tae kwon do." His head shakes for a moment, like he's trying to rattle the answer free from memory before he continues. "Anyway, I skipped out on the lesson and went exploring the neighborhood with Billie. She was always running around, doing whatever she wanted and I was always a little jealous of that, so I joined in. Well, what Billie wanted to do that day was go into a foreclosed home and see what we could find. I ended up cutting the back of my hand on a rusty metal cabinet." He shrugs a shoulder and smiles at me. "Seemed like a good idea at the time."

I return the smile, but it doesn't quite reach my eyes as I continue to trace the scar with my finger. "When was the last time you did something for you?" I ask, noticing Jake's smile fall and his brow furrow. "Even when you were ditching plans, it was to do something Billie wanted to do, and coming here this time was her idea, so…" I don't want to ruin the mood, but I need to make sure he's here because he wants to be, not because he's following someone else's idea of what he should be doing.

Jake holds the back of my head in a gesture that is both sweet and possessive. "I need you to understand something, Beautiful. No one makes me do anything I don't want to do," he tells me, his gaze intense and unwavering. "And what I want to do is be with you. Not out of a sense of obligation because you are the mother of my child, not because of a wish either of us made in a fountain, but because you are the strongest, most caring, most capable, and most outright amazing person I have ever met." He rests his forehead against mine and sighs. "I love you, Maya. Wild horses couldn't drag me away from here."

His words are a balm on my battered heart, and I let the last of my doubts slip away. Cupping his jaw, enjoying the feel of his freshly shaved skin against my palm, I take a shuddering breath. "I love you too," I tell him, letting the feel of him ground me. "I have loved you since the moment we locked eyes in the store three years ago."

"Me too, Beautiful. Me too," Jake breathes out. His lips feather across mine before pulling back. His expression is so affectionate, but I see the fire blazing underneath. I squirm a little in my seat, a hunger that has nothing to do with our meal taking over, the need to be with him getting out of control again. One look in his eyes lets me know he feels it too.

Jake raises a hand to flag down our waiter and switches our meal to takeout. He glances over at me, a mischievous smile on his face. "I hope you're okay if we speed things along a little. I know I promised you a date, but I find I'm not in the mood to be in public at the moment."

I reach over and grab the upper half of his thigh and give it a squeeze, swirling my fingers suggestively. "Fine by me," I tell him. My voice is husky with desire, and I smile wickedly as his head lolls back and he shifts in his chair.

"You're a menace," he growls, but he doesn't tell me to move my hand. I continue to knead the strong muscle of his leg as we wait for our food. Once it's at the table, Jake tosses a few hundred-dollar bills on the table and grabs our coats and the food boxes. "Let's go, Beautiful."

Giggling like a schoolgirl, I stand up with him and walk out the door. I'm so worked up and my skin is so heated that I barely feel the cold air on my skin as we head to the car. When we get there, I laugh as Jake unceremoniously dumps everything in the back seat before opening my door for me. "You in a hurry? I got a sitter, remember," I tell him, stepping into his space and leaning up on my tiptoes to whisper in his ear. "We have all night."

Jake's chest rumbles and I smile as he lightly swats my behind. "Don't I know it? Now get in, Beautiful. I plan on using every minute of our night to my advantage." With that and a swift but fierce kiss on my lips, Jake helps me into the car and runs around to his side. We simply stare at each other for a moment, a swirl of emotions surrounding us. Finally, he starts the car and heads back to his place, and for me, the time cannot go by fast enough.

Chapter Twenty
Jake

The drive to the rental was mercifully short, though it could never be short enough after hearing Maya tell me she loved me. When she spoke those sweet words in my ear, my heart nearly beat out of my chest and I wanted nothing more than to make love to her right then and there. I was happy to see she was on the same page, but I don't think either of us wanted an audience. As quickly and as inconspicuously as possible, I got us out of the restaurant. There was also the desire to not embarrass myself by coming in my pants as she rubbed her hand up and down my thigh. The slightest touch from her sets my skin on fire and as much as I liked what she was doing, I was happy she had to stop when we no longer had the privacy a tablecloth was providing.

Now we're alone at last, and after letting Maya into the cabin, I practically kick the door shut before moving to the small kitchen in the rental and dropping off the food boxes and our coats. When I turn back and look over at my beautiful girl, her eyes are hooded and she's kicking off her boots, nodding for me to do the same. "Normally, I would try to tease this out a little, try to be a little sexier, make it last, but I'm too far gone for that," she says with a shrug of her shoulder. Her hands reach the hem of her sweater and whip it off and over her head. My eyes rake up and down her creamy-looking skin, my mouth watering, itching to get a taste of it. The sound of a zipper has my attention going south and I move my eyes there just in time to see a hint of pink peeking out from between the open window of her jeans. She lowers them to the floor and kicks them aside, sauntering over to me. "You're a few steps behind, Love."

The word "love" has me floating on cloud nine, but her hands snaking their way underneath my sweater brings me crashing back down to earth. I smirk as I look down at the woman in front of me. "Think you could help me out with that, Beautiful?"

Maya nods, a playful smile on her face. "I will gladly help with anything that involves you in less clothes." Her warm hands skim over my chest for a moment before shoving my sweater up and over my head while I toe off my shoes and drop my pants. Maya steps back so I can kick them to the side, and when my gaze meets hers, her expression is one of barely restrained want as she takes in the tent of my boxer briefs. She makes a whimpering sound as she stares before finally snapping back to it and reaching behind her back to unclasp her bra. When it drops to the floor, I nearly follow along with it, wanting to drop to my knees to pay homage to her gorgeous breasts. They are bigger than before. I should know because I spent half that first night together searing every inch of her body into my memory banks. God, I need to get my hands and mouth on them again.

"Fuck," I whisper. Reaching over, I pull her closer to me so I can press her body up against mine. "You are beautiful in so many ways, but this body is unreal." I run a hand up her side until I can run my thumb under her breast. "I cannot wait to spend the rest of the night worshipping every inch of you."

Maya looks into my eyes, a fire beneath the icy-blue depths of her own. "Don't tell me, show me," she commands, before she pulls my mouth to hers for a kiss. We don't even make a pit stop at sweet and take the kiss directly to sultry and sizzling, my desire amplifying with each pass of her lips. Maya drives into my mouth, sucking on my tongue so hard I'm spilling pre-cum in my briefs. Her other hand moves to grip my ass and I buck into her, a whimper sounding against my mouth. It could be her or me, I'm not sure. The only thing I know is that the whimpering soon turns into moans as I tweak one of her nipples with my thumb and forefinger and she kneads my behind. We continue to explore each other's bodies, getting reacquainted with what's familiar and what's different. She's a little softer from pregnancy and giving birth, and I'm a little harder from having nothing better to do than work out, but the changes don't matter. We're still a perfect fit. Finally, it's Maya who breaks the kiss. "Need you," she breathes out. Seconds later, she's diving back, nipping and sucking at my lower lip while our bodies press against each other.

I moan my agreement and let her lead me over to the bed, flopping backward when she pushes me down. A wide smile pulls across my face as I scoot back and she strips off the last of her clothes. Her inhibitions and lack of confidence from earlier this week have melted away as she stands in front of me as the proud and beautiful Viking goddess she is. Maya tosses her panties to the side before crawling up on the bed, running her hands up my legs until finally she's grasping the waistband of my briefs. She raises a brow in question, and I'm nodding so fast I'm surprised my head doesn't pop off. "Do it," I tell her. I'm loving the look on her face as she shucks my underpants and flings them behind her, but I love her even more and I can't wait to express that with more than just words.

Maya smirks and crawls back up, and I close my eyes and wait for her to come kiss me again, but that doesn't happen. Instead, all the air leaves my body in a giant whoosh as I feel her mouth close over my rock-hard cock. "Fuck, Beautiful. What are you doing?" I was supposed to be spoiling her, not the other way around.

Maya pops off me with a frown on her face. "Did you not want me to?"

I huff a laugh. "Um, no, I definitely want you to, but I want to give you what you need first." I always want to give her what she needs if it's in my power to do so.

The frown leaves Maya's face as she grips my base with one hand while teasing my balls with the other. "This is what I need," she says before she teasingly licks the head with the tip of her pink tongue. "And what I want." She takes all of me in one move and any protest at what she is doing flies away in the face of just how good her hot mouth feels. Maya continues to bob up and down, working me with her hands and sucking on me like I'm the tastiest lollipop that has ever been invented as I lightly stroke the side of her face, amazed once again at just how much this woman gives of herself without expecting anything in return.

After another couple of minutes of her amazing mouth skills and me feeling like my body will burst into flames, I feel myself getting close. Too close. The need to come is so strong, but I want our first time back together to be about more than my own pleasure. "Gotta stop," I grit out, feeling relief only after Maya halts what she's doing.

Soon, she's hovering above me, the silky strands of her hair cascading down in waves. "Why didn't you let me finish?" she asks with a pout. While I would like nothing more than to suck that full lip of hers into my mouth, I need to back away from the edge and that certainly won't help.

I chuckle lightly. "Turn that frown upside down, Beautiful. You can do that to me wherever and whenever you want in the future, but right now I want to play a little too." Gripping her hips and giving them a squeeze, I roll us so she's on her back and I'm on top, my body settled between her long legs. Leaning down, I kiss her plump lips one more time before trailing my kisses south along her cheek, jaw, and neck. When I get to her chest, I cradle one breast in my hand, flicking her nipple with my thumb as my mouth latches onto the other, sucking and nipping as her body writhes beneath mine. I do this for a while, honestly loving it and thinking I could easily set up camp right here, but I won't. I pop off her breast, smiling wickedly as I switch sides and go after the other one. Maya is a mewling mess beneath me, her hands tangled in my curls as she arches her back, begging me for more with her actions. Nothing has ever looked as good as the sight of her being pleased by me.

"Jake," she whines. Her hips grind against me as she tries to get the friction she needs so badly. "Need you inside me. Please."

I stop my ministrations and move above her face, leaning down to kiss her breathless once more. "No need for please, Love. You can order me around any way you want."

I slide my hips up and line myself with her center. After running my dick through her wet folds a few times, making sure to hit that sweet spot at the top, I stop, suddenly remembering my trip to the convenience store last night. "Shit," I grit out. My body is desperately wanting to drive into her hard and deep, but my mind knows we need protection. I rest my head against her chest. "I haven't been with anyone since you, so I'm clean. Condoms are in the nightstand."

Maya cups my cheeks and brings my gaze back up to hers. "I haven't been with anyone since you either. I'm clean and have an IUD." She smiles at me, laughter in her eyes. "Forgive me if I no longer trust the reliability of condoms."

I chuckle and lean down to kiss her, but a moan escapes my mouth before I can. My eyes move down to where Maya is gripping onto my dick again, rubbing it against her clit. "Fuck, that is so hot," I admit as I desperately try not to come.

"You said I was the boss, so get inside me now before I use just the tip to get what I need," she tells me. She is attempting to smirk, but it fails when she gasps and cries out after I drive myself into her in one swift move.

I smile and grind into her as hard as I can, watching her for any signals that it's too much. "I said you could order me around, Beautiful, but I'm still the boss," I tell her. My hips snap back and push in again, deeper this time to try and hit that magic spot inside that will have her crying out my name over and over again. Nothing feels as good as being with her like this, and I can't wait to spend the rest of our lives making love as often as possible.

My thrusts go deeper until I bottom out. Our bodies are as close as two bodies can get without melting into one another, though the way we move together, so in sync, feels as if we are at least sharing the same brain if not the same body. Maya's hands move up my back until she's gripping my shoulders, her heels digging into my ass as I piston in and out of her. I angle my hips until I see her eyes start to roll back inside her head. "There we go." I sigh. Sweat breaks out over my body from the exertion of holding myself above her, and I drive myself inside of her, trying to stave off my own orgasm for as long as I can.

A low moan escapes Maya's mouth as her hands scratch my back. "So good," she pants out. "So, so good. I think I'm—" her words cut off as her eyes light up. Watching her chase and capture her orgasm has to be the most stunning thing I have ever seen, like catching lightning in a bottle. I keep going, wanting to get her there again, and when she cries out a little louder, the sound ringing out through the room, I finally give in to the tingling at the base of my spine and follow along with her, my eyes never leaving hers as I grunt out my release.

When we're both sweaty and spent, I roll off to the side and gather her in my arms, enjoying the feeling of having her there and loving that this will be the first of many nights together. Our future isn't completely secure yet, but what is secure is my knowing that no matter what, we'll make it work so the two of us can be together along with our son. I love her and I love JJ. No matter what comes of my business proposal next week, I'm never leaving them behind again.

Maya's contented sigh next to me makes me smile, and I lean over to kiss her temple. "God, I missed that," she breathes out. Her blue eyes meet mine, and she smiles. "It's been a long time since we were together, but it felt just like it did last time, like your body could read mine so well and give me exactly what it needed." She shakes her head and hides her face in my chest. "That probably sounds so dumb."

"No," I tell her, lifting her gaze back to mine. "It sounds exactly like it felt to me. It was like you were in my mind, my body, my soul. You were everywhere and it was amazing and crazy and magic all at the same time."

Maya smiles shyly and leans over, brushing her lips against mine. "I'm going to clean up a little and then what do you say to some cold ratatouille and roast chicken?"

I kiss her once more, loving that I can touch her as freely as I want now. No interruptions, no holding back out of fear, nothing keeping us apart. "I say let's eat in bed so as soon as I have a little strength back we can start round two."

Maya smiles and nods. "Sounds like a plan," she says. As I watch her leave the bed and wander over to the bathroom in all her naked glory, I decide that is one plan I'm going to stick to.

Chapter Twenty-One
Maya

The sound of geese honking brings me out of a peaceful night's sleep. It's not the sound of geese honking that's unfamiliar to me, but the feel of cool, cotton sheets underneath me that has me slightly confused. In the fall and winter, I am exclusively a flannel sheets kind of gal, so I know I'm not at home. Waking up in a bed other than my own is so foreign to me that it takes me a few moments before I remember where I am and who I am with. With a contented sigh, I reach over for Jake only to come up empty-handed. The same sense of loss I felt all those years ago returns, an old familiar visitor that you'd rather never come around again.

Shaking that feeling off and squinting one eye open, I peek around the room, knowing I'll find Jake around here somewhere. I trust Jake to not leave, I think it might just take my body a while to catch up with my brain and heart when it comes to pushing the panic aside. My eyes roam over the wood paneling, noting the nature photography and macramé on the walls. It should look outdated, but it's tastefully done and I make a mental reminder to ask the cabin's owners who supplied the décor. It could be a good find for the store. Finally, my eyes roam over to the kitchenette and land on Jake, seeing him staring into an open cabinet and frowning intently.

"What is in that cabinet that could have personally offended you so much?" I ask, my voice slightly raspy from sleep. My body twists as my limbs stretch out the remnants of sleep and I yawn. My muscles are deliciously sore from rounds one through three last night and round four in the wee hours of the morning, and I can't wait for more rounds over the coming days, weeks, months, and years. Knowing we have years ahead of us brings a wide smile to my face, a smile which only widens when Jake shucks his sweats and climbs back into bed with me.

"There is nothing in that cabinet but instant coffee and some stale crackers," he says with a frustrated grunt. Reaching over, he pulls my back to his front and wraps a strong arm around my middle. "I was hoping to make you breakfast in bed, but I forgot that I've been spending most of my time at your place, so there's nothing here."

I wiggle my ass into his hardening length, smiling when he groans and reaches a hand up to cup my breast. "I can think of a few ways we can take our minds off breakfast for a little while."

Jake presses himself against me as he peppers kisses across my shoulder. "I like the way you think, Beautiful, but I want to take care of you."

My heart melts at his declaration, but what I need from him right now has nothing to do with food. Our connection is strong when we're doing nothing at all, but it feels even stronger when we're together in bed and I need that right now. After three years without it, I need it more than I need anything else. The closeness, the intimacy of it all, is like a drug and I need another hit. With a steady hand, I move his hand from my breast down to my clit and start rubbing myself against it. "You are taking care of me," I assure him. Pressing three of his fingers inside me, an almost obscene moan escapes from my mouth as I move against his hand. His fingers are long and thick, filling me up just enough to have my breath hitching with each movement.

"This what you need, Beautiful? Need me to get you off again?" he asks. I nod, the back of my head hitting his shoulder as he curls his fingers, hitting that elusive spot deep inside that he seems to be able to find in seconds. Jake hums softly against my hair. "Love doing this for you. And I plan on doing it every chance I get."

"Sounds good to…" I agree before a gasp breaks off my words. Jake's thumb is thrumming over my clit, and the added sensation has my body tensing, readying itself for my orgasm. I reach a hand back and lace it in his copper curls, tugging when he hits just the right pressure and speed to have me close. "Jake."

"I know, Beautiful. Come for me," he commands. Almost instantly the tension I've been feeling in my body tightens and releases, and a warm euphoria floods through my body as a silent cry leaves my throat. As soon as I come down from my high, I feel Jake pull his fingers out only to lick them clean. "Damn. You taste just as good as I remember."

I chuckle breathlessly as I return to my body. "Of all the things to remember," I say, spinning around and looking into his deep-blue eyes.

Jake lightly brushes my hair away from my face. "I remember everything," he whispers. He looks so completely in love with me that I can't catch my breath from feeling like the most special woman that ever lived. I need him again, not just for release, but to feel that sense of connection and devotion I crave whenever he looks at me the way he is now. Pushing Jake onto his back and climbing on top of him, I notice he's still hard. Since I am more than ready, I line myself up and impale myself on him in one move, swirling my hips and leaning down to press our lips together. Jake's hands immediately move over my body. Gripping my hips and ass before moving up to rub my back. My hips slant as I search for the right angle, and when I find it, I grind my body against his over and over again until Jake breaks the kiss, panting for air. "God, you're amazing," he tells me. He's gritting his teeth as I bring him closer to the edge, and the knowledge that I'm the one giving him this pleasure has me preening.

"*We're* amazing," I correct him, breathing heavily as I feel the telltale signs of another orgasm coming upon me. As soon as Jake leans up and pinches one of my nipples, I am done for, moaning and coming harder than I have in a very long time. Jake comes just after me, thrusting his hips up to meet mine as he spills inside me. Collapsing on his chest from all the effort, I rest my head on his shoulder and lightly brush my fingers through the springy hair between his pectorals as he comes down with me.

One of Jake's hands is splayed on my back while the other is running through my hair. "Thank you," he tells me, kissing my temple.

"For the sex?" I ask wryly. "Because if you plan on thanking me each time, you might get tired of saying it." Now that we're together again, I know I am going to want him at least twice a day if not more, though I have a feeling a certain two-year-old will put a kink in those plans soon enough.

Jake snorts and shakes his head. "I am happy to hear that you want to do this more often, but I wasn't thanking you for the sex, though it was pretty spectacular."

I feel my grin widen as I rest my chin on his chest. "It was." The most spectacular I have ever had. While I don't have a lot of points of reference, I know for sure that no one has ever made me feel as cherished as Jake, and no one has ever made me feel like my bones have been liquefied either.

Jake returns my smile and continues to brush his hand through my hair. "I was thanking you for everything," he says, his gaze serious. "I'm so glad I stopped for lunch that day three years ago."

"Me too," I tell him, reaching up to give him a kiss. When I move back, the charm around my neck is resting against his lightly freckled skin.

His fingers reach down and trace along the three interconnected triangles of the valknut charm. "Family," he breathes out reverently.

I nod and cup his face. "Family," I tell him. My thumb traces his lower lip as it pulls into a small smile. He and JJ are my family now, and I plan on treating them with just as much respect and importance as I have my other family. "You know, the night we met, I wished to have a sense of family again. And it happened, just not exactly the way I thought it would."

Jake smiles and brushes his lips lightly against mine. "I wished for something extraordinary to happen." He rests his forehead against mine and I relax into him, our bodies messing together. "I guess both our wishes came true," he says, leaning in to kiss me. As we once again lose ourselves in the pleasure of being with one another, there is also the wonderful feeling that we are creating something new together, something permanent, and something even more extraordinary than what we already have.

****

The week leading up to Jake leaving to go back to Denver goes by way too fast. We spent as much time together as possible while also trying to squeeze in time for Jake and Billie to work on his presentation as well as time for Billie to get to know JJ. While I'm sure there isn't a man alive who wouldn't flock to Billie's side in an instant, JJ just didn't feel the same way about her. She tried everything from attempting to play with him to bribing him with sweets, but nothing worked. I felt a little bad, but she shrugged it off, saying she can handle a man who plays hard to get, a comment which earned a snort from Jake and a chuckle from me.

When she wasn't helping Jake or attempting to bond with my son, Billie was in the workshop out back, trying to annoy my brother. If the perma-scowl he's been wearing all week is any indication, she succeeded. Personally, I think he's jealous of her ability to flit around from person to person and make conversation so easily, but I can't be sure. She left yesterday, so I tried to bring up the topic, but he redirected the conversation to something else. I've decided to leave it alone for now, but something tells me it won't be the last time the topic of Billie comes up between my brother and me.

Trying to sneak in a few moments with just Jake and me has been difficult as well, especially with a two-year-old and my brother in the same apartment. It's not like I wanted to ask Carter to babysit every night just so Jake and I could have sex, or even would if I had the inclination. That wouldn't be fair to my brother. A woman has needs, though, so Jake and I have had to get a little creative. We have been able to sneak in a couple of quickies while JJ takes a nap in the other room, but it's not nearly enough. I want to be able to really spend quality time exploring my man, but I'll take what I can get. Especially since he's taking off this morning. I know he's coming back, I'm just not sure under what circumstances. Maybe his presentation will go well and he'll be moving here, or maybe it will go sideways and we have to figure out a long-distance thing. Or maybe JJ and I can move to Denver. I don't love the idea of leaving my little mountain town or Carter, but I would do it if it meant our small family could be together.

"I wish you didn't have to go," I tell Jake. Next to

me, he holds tightly onto JJ, getting in as much cuddle time as our little boy will allow. He used to be content with playing in the office, but since Jake has shown up, he's been more curious about exploring. One look at our son tells me he's going to miss his new playmate just as much as Jake is going to miss him.

Jake tries to smooth out JJ's curls, a losing battle as they spring back no matter what you do, and smiles sadly at me. "I know, Beautiful. I wish I didn't have to go either." He kisses JJ on the cheek. "I'll see you soon, okay, bud?"

"Okay," JJ tells him. He pats Jake's cheeks with each hand a few times before wiggling to be put down. He toddles over to the office and starts playing with his blocks, completely unaware of the gravity of the situation in front of us. I'm not unaware, and my heart is heavy with thoughts of things possibly not working out.

Before he even has his arms extended, I step into Jake and hug his chest, holding him as tightly as I can while breathing in his forest scent. It's comforting, and I might have to get an air freshener for my room to help me feel better while he's gone. "I love you," I get out over a sniffle.

Jake hugs me tightly for a moment and sways me from side to side, comforting me in a way I often use on JJ when he's upset. It's soothing and I wish we could just stay like this all day. Finally, he pulls back and wipes away the stray tear from my face. "Don't cry," he says, sealing his mouth over mine in a searing goodbye kiss. "I love you too, Maya." His brow is furrowed, but his look is determined. "I will come back to you. JJ is my heart, and you are my soul, my home. You are my everything, Beautiful. Everything."

Emotion clogs my throat, so I simply nod my agreement, not sure I can even speak now. After one more hug, I step back and find my voice enough to wish him luck. "Will you let me know how it goes?"

"Absolutely," he says. His expression is hopeful, but I can see the anxiety on his face too. Knowing he wants this just as badly as I do helps, but I'm still nervous something is going to keep him from coming back. It's like déjà vu of the worst kind, and I wish we could just fast-forward to the end where he comes back to us.

With one last glance into the office at our son, Jake steps back and heads toward the front door. Before he leaves, he turns and looks at me. "This isn't goodbye, Maya. I will come home."

A shaky smile comes over my face and I will my nerves to calm down. "I know." I do know he will come back, but having the confidence to feel it is still new. "See you soon."

Jake smiles and nods, finally leaving the store. Watching him walk away is hard, but I just keep reminding myself that he is coming home. I trust him and I trust in our love for one another. This whole thing may have started with a wish, a hope whispered into the wind for something special knowing it might never come true, but now it's about something else. It's about trusting that what we have is real, solid, and isn't going anywhere.

Chapter Twenty-Two
Jake

The drive back to Denver yesterday was brutal, and not just because it started to snow heavily about a half hour outside of Starlight Lake. The drive felt like an exercise in discipline, my knuckles white as I gripped the steering wheel and willed myself to keep going. My mind kept rationalizing the trip. It was what was best, I was working on something that would get me there permanently, so I had to keep going regardless of the fact it felt like I had carved my heart out and left it behind. At one point, I seriously considered just quitting my job, turning around, and working as a part-time lumberjack or whatever other available work I could find so I wouldn't have to spend one more day away from Maya and JJ. Ultimately, I kept going, trying to focus on what was best in the long term. My heart could ache for a few days while I waited to return to them. It had three years of practice, so hopefully it wouldn't be that bad.

It had been that bad, though. Returning to my cold and lifeless apartment felt awful. Where were JJ's blocks? Why weren't Maya's crochet hooks and yarn scattered about? Where was the sense of home I had found with the woman I felt tethered to more than anything else in this world? Home was a few hours west with the people I love, and they were counting on me to do my best and come back to them. It's something I told myself repeatedly as I tossed in a fitful sleep in my bed, getting almost no rest at all.

Luckily for me, my always cheery assistant, Kendall, appears with a cup of espresso the moment I step off the elevator into the offices of Mile High Consulting. "You are a godsend," I tell him. I start walking and sip the hot liquid, enjoying the robust flavor and making a note to make sure I take some of this coffee with me when I go back home. Thinking of Maya and JJ as my home once again brings a smile to my face, and when I glance at my assistant, he's a little teary eyed. "Kendall, what's wrong?"

He waves off my question and sniffles. "Nothing," he says. He pulls a pocket square out of his shirt and dabs at his eyes. "You just look so happy."

I nod as we walk into what will hopefully soon be my former office. "I am happy. Very happy, actually." I polish off the coffee in record time and place the empty cup on my desk. After starting up my computer, I give Kendall a nod and ask him to sit. "What did you think of my plan?" One of the many calls I made during my time away was to Kendall to update him on the situation and get his take on my business proposal. He's a hard worker and whip smart, so I value his opinion highly.

Kendall clasps both hands gracefully on his knee and straightens his posture. "I thought it was good." His eyes flick away for a moment, a tell of his that says he's lying. When I glare at him, he shrugs. "I don't know what you want me to say. The idea has merit, but I just don't see the need to open a satellite office. Especially one where you don't have an assistant," he says, sounding slightly irritated.

"Ah." Now I know why he seems upset. "I should have made this clearer in the proposal, but you would still be my assistant, Kendall, just a virtual one," I explain. "Unless of course you want to move to Starlight Lake."

Kendall scoffs. "Please. I'm a city boy through and through," he insists haughtily. "I am happy to accept the virtual assistant position, though." His eyes brighten and he claps his hands. "Does this mean I get to work from home?"

I chuckle and nod. "It would be hybrid with a few days in the office now and then, but yes, mostly from home."

Kendall stands and offers up a hand. "Deal," he says happily. "You better do well on this presentation. Don't screw this up for me." He points to me as sternly as his mostly sunny personality will allow.

"Of course," I tell him with a curt nod. "You getting to work from home is clearly my top priority here." With a smile, Kendall exits my office just as Billie saunters in, looking much more professional that she usually does in a dark pantsuit, her hair in a tight bun.

"What's with the getup?" I ask, waving my hand in her uncharacteristically modest attire. "Are you attending a funeral later?"

"Har-har," she says, sitting across from me. "I came for moral support and thought it best to look as boring as possible so as to not detract from your presentation."

"Mission accomplished," I tell her, smiling when she rolls her eyes and flips me off. She may not be as spoiled and vain as she put on, but she does still care about her appearance, so I know my good-natured jab hit its mark. The alarm on my phone chimes, letting me know I have exactly ten minutes to get my ass upstairs to the executive conference room to set up.

Billie slaps her thighs and stands with me. "You ready to do this?"

"As ready as I'll ever be," I tell her, gathering my laptop and printed materials Kendall set out on my desk. As we pass by my assistant, he grins and gives me a thumbs-up. I return his enthusiastic smile and nod, but when my gaze turns to Billie, the smile slips off my face. She looks upset and I'm not sure why. "Hey, what's going on?"

"What? Nothing." Billie mashes the elevator button harder than necessary. She continues to mash the button while mumbling curse words at it. Reaching over, I still her hand and give her a searching look. With a sigh, she drops her hand and looks at me, a pained expression on her face. "I want this to go well for you. I want you to get to be with Maya and JJ," she says, shrugging a shoulder. "I'm just going to miss having you around."

My brow furrows. In all of this, I hadn't really thought about my best friend and how she would feel about everything. She's been endlessly supportive of me and I haven't thought about her once. Guilt trickles in and tightens my chest. I feel like such a jerk. "I'm going to miss having you around too," I tell her, pulling her in for a hug. "You can come out and visit whenever you want. We're only a few hours away."

"I guess," Billie says. The sound is muffled against my chest as we continue to hug it out. When she pulls back, the pained look is gone, replaced by a devilish gleam in her eye. "Coming for a visit and annoying Carter could be fun."

My head leans back on an exasperated sigh as we enter the recently arrived lift. "Why do you insist on annoying the man? He's just trying to do his job."

"I don't know. It's fun," Billie offers. Her head turns away from me, but not before I catch the slight blush on her cheeks.

While I could warn her away from Carter again, I don't see it being much of an issue with them living so far apart. Billie will probably move on from whatever weird fascination she has with him and onto something else soon enough. I don't really have the mental space to think about all this anyway, so I let it go. Right now, I need to walk into that conference room and crush this presentation.

****

The view from my windshield never looked as good as it does now. In the near distance, I can see Starlight Lake and the sense of peace that fills me is unimaginable. Soon I will be back with my family, and not just temporarily. The presentation went better than expected. Both my father and Billie's agreed that I could easily do my current work remotely and loved the idea of setting up a small business wing of the firm, using my work in Starlight Lake and the surrounding areas as a pilot program. It will mean a good amount of groundwork on my part, but it will be worth it to be able to be with Maya and JJ.

As I make the turn toward downtown, the suitcases and boxes in the back of my SUV shift slightly, banging against the window. They are filled with everything I will need to get by until I have a more permanent place to live while everything else sits in storage in Denver. Breaking the lease on my apartment was a no-brainer and totally worth the cost to be able to leave as quickly as possible. What was less easy was saying goodbye to my parents and Billie. I'll see them when I travel to Denver once every other month, but it will be different, especially for Billie. She insists she'll be fine, but I'm a little worried about her getting lonely. I wasn't one for the party scene, but we still had lunches, dinners, and hung out at my place all the time. Hopefully, one of the many other friends she has will step up and keep her company.

Finally, the sight I have been waiting three days to see comes into view and a wide grin spreads across my face as I pull into a spot in front of Hodgepodge. The night I told Maya I was coming home for good, she shrieked into the phone so loudly I had to hold the speaker away from my ear for a second, laughing in giddy happiness along with her as we talked about my plans and all the details we still had to hammer out. As I walk into the store, my eyes immediately spot Maya as she shows JJ how to dust the shelves lightly. We talked every night on the phone, but I still missed the two of them like crazy. Maya's back is turned to me, so I try to sneak up on the two of them. Before I can surprise Maya, JJ peeks out and spots me. "Daddy," he exclaims before rushing over to me. Maya spins around, her eyes wide and happy as I lift our little boy into my arms and hold him close.

"Hey, bud," I choke out. All the emotions I'm experiencing has my tongue feeling thicker than usual, so I'm surprised I got those words out at all. It's the first time he's called me Daddy. This moment will live in my mind forever, and I don't think I'll ever get over hearing my son call me that. My heart is filled with happiness as I cuddle my boy impossibly closer. "I missed you."

"Miss oo, Daddy," JJ tells me, wiggling in his arms until I let him down. He runs over to the office and Maya steps into the space he just occupied.

"I'm so glad you're back," she says in greeting. Upon seeing her and feeling her so close to me, I can take my first full breath of the last three days.

"Glad to be back, Beautiful." I lean down and kiss her. It only lasts a moment, but that's all I need to feel our connection strengthening again. JJ comes crashing back into my legs and holds a picture frame up for me. I grab onto it and look, the image starting to blur slightly from the moisture that gathers in my eyes. The frame says, "Daddy and Me," and inside is a picture of he and I that Maya must have taken when I wasn't looking. JJ's head rests on my shoulder as I hold him, and the two of us look so relaxed and comfortable with one another that it takes me a moment to realize it's from one of the first days I was here. I reach down and pick JJ up once more. "This is great, bud. I love it."

"It's for your office," Maya says, a shy smile on her face. "Whenever you get one, that is."

"This is amazing. I love it," I tell her, leaning over and kissing her once more. "Now I need one of you." I can't wait to decorate whatever space I work in with pictures and photos of the two most important people in the world to me.

Maya smirks, her cheeks turning pink. "Oh. I, uh, have a couple of pictures for you," she says, her eyes lighting up. "Maybe not for your office, though."

My chest rumbles with the need to be with her, but the little boy in my arms works as a good libido killer. "Show me later," I command.

"Absolutely," she tells me with a wink. "Until then, what would you like to do? The store closes in an hour. Should we go out to dinner to celebrate?"

I nod, gathering her close so my arms are filled with nothing but the people I love. "We can do whatever we want, Beautiful. We have all the time in the world." This time, we actually do, and I plan on using every minute of that time making sure the two people next to me know just how much I love and care for them. Three years ago I wished for something extraordinary. What I ended up with was that, and a whole lot more.

Epilogue
Maya

Three Months Later

The weather on Valentine's Day in Starlight Lake can go one of two ways. It's either cold, or unbearably cold. Unfortunately, it's the latter for mine and Jake's first time celebrating the holiday together. Even at midday, the temperature is in single digits. As cold as it is, though, it's still the best Valentine's Day I have ever had. The day started off well with Jake and me taking a shower together at the apartment. It was close quarters, but we made it work as we got each other off as quietly as possible as to not disturb our two roommates as they slept. We've been looking to get a bigger place, but real estate in Starlight Lake can be tricky since there isn't a lot of new construction going on, especially in the dead of winter. Still, we've managed to make it work, though having to go back to the old sock on the doorknob trick with my brother was a bit weird. To his credit, Carter never brings it up, simply takes JJ for a car ride or to the library until I text him the all-clear. It's not a perfect system, but it works for now.

After our antics in the shower this morning, Jake went off to work at the office share a few blocks down from Hodgepodge for a couple of hours. It works out well because he doesn't have to pay for a whole office and he's close enough to come have lunch with JJ and me. His work is going well, though he hopes to be able to cut down on working even the few hours on weekends. The other day I asked him if he wished he had his old schedule back, and he looked at me like I'd sprouted another head. "Not if it means I don't have you," he had said. Then he kissed me until I was certain his words were true.

After he was done with work, Jake brought me a dozen roses before taking me out to lunch. Carter took over in the shop and watched JJ so we could spend some time together. I feel a little bad asking my brother to babysit all the time, but he insists he loves it and wants to give Jake and me as much time together as possible. My brother really is the most thoughtful guy, and I hope he finds a person of his own soon. He won't admit it, but I know Carter wants to be in a relationship, he's just afraid to try. I get it, relationships are tough, but even dealing with three years of uncertainty was worth it to have what I do now. A man who loves me and a wonderful little boy who is the apple of our eyes.

Lunch was as romantic as possible for having eaten at Fran's Place. Business owners from up and down the block insisted on coming over a little too often to visit with Jake and me. I love all the people in the community, but I was hoping for more privacy. Mercifully, we're alone now, driving around in the car and taking in the scenic views of the town. Looking at our joined hands resting on the center console, I smile and give Jake's a squeeze. "Thanks for today. I can't say I have a whole lot of experience with Valentine's Day, but this was definitely a good one."

Jake pulls my hand up to his to kiss it. "It's about to get even better," he tells me. There is a slightly nervous expression on his face as he pulls into a driveway.

My eyes peer out the window and widen as I look at the same house I spent most of my life in. "Jake. What are we doing here?" It's still the same sad color it was the last time I saw it, and if this is some kind of revisit-the-past moment, I'm not sure I'm up for it after seeing how neglected the house has been.

Jake gives me a meaningful look and flips my palm over before dropping a key into it. My eyes widen as they shoot up to his. "Hopefully, righting a wrong and starting a new chapter all at the same time."

My fingers tighten around the metal of the key, the ridges digging into my skin slightly. "What are you talking about?" I practically whisper, both excited and afraid to know the answer.

"I'll show you," he says, exiting the vehicle and coming over to my side to help me out. My legs feel like jelly and my knees are weak, but somehow I manage to make it up the steps to the porch and slip the key inside the lock. What I can't manage is turning it. I haven't stepped foot anywhere near this house since we sold it, and I'm not sure I'm strong enough to handle the flood of emotions that's likely to come along if I do. "I-I can't."

Jake places one hand over mine and cups my face with the other. "If you really can't, we can turn around and I will sell this place and we can buy something else." He looks deeply into my eyes and I see how much he cares and how he would absolutely turn around and sell a house he specifically bought just for me. "But I think you're strong enough to face whatever it is you're afraid of, and I know how much this house means to you."

"It did ... it does mean a lot to me," I stammer out. He's right. If I don't at least look around, I'll regret it. "Okay." After taking a deep breath, I unlock the door and step inside. My eyes move around the space, noting what's changed. It's not dank and dusty like I imagined it would be, but it does look a little different. A few paint colors here and some new light fixtures there are all signs that the house is not what it used to be, but instead of making me sad, I'm happy that someone came in and made this house their own, gave it life when I wasn't able to. Now, I can do the same. Turning to Jake, I grasp his hand and hold it tightly. "Thank you for this. I can't believe you bought it. I didn't even know it was for sale."

He shrugs a shoulder. "It wasn't," he admits, looking at me sheepishly. "Turns out when you offer a good deal of money over the current value, people are pretty motivated to sell." I open my mouth to protest the expense, but Jake silences me with a knowing look. "It's just money, Maya. Something we still have plenty of, and not anywhere near an amount that would ever put us in a position to lose this place again."

"Okay." The words whoosh out of me along with any anxiety I was feeling. Jake shared the state of his finances with me, so I know he's good for the money. Still, it's hard to break the habit of worrying about what things cost when you've had to for a good number of years. I release his hand and walk into the family room, running my hand along the wood mantel my father created, dipping my fingers along the woodland scene he carved into the front. "Jake, you have to come see this."

When I spin around to look for him, he's already right in front of me, but he isn't standing, he's down on one knee. A small gasp escapes my mouth we he reaches for my hand. "Maya, my beautiful, amazing, magical Maya. I love you with every part of me and I always will. I never want to spend another moment without you or our son. I want us to be a family. Officially." He smiles nervously. "Will you marry me?"

Nodding through the happy tears, I finally manage to squeak out a "yes" as he slips a sapphire engagement ring on my finger. Jake stands and gathers me into his arms. "I love you so much," I tell him before reaching up to kiss him, putting all the love and affection I feel for him into it. "I'm so glad I made that wish."

Jake smiles and brushes his lips against mine. "I'm glad it came true," he says.

Even though the road to our happily ever after was a rocky one, I wouldn't have it any other way because it led us to this moment. A moment I will remember for the rest of my life.

The End

SYDNEY SCOTT

EVERNIGHT PUBLISHING ®

www.evernightpublishing.com